About the Author

Paul Devito studied philosophy and literature in graduate school and has devoted his life to writing and painting.

The Wind and the Rain

Paul Devito

The Wind and the Rain

Olympia Publishers
London

www.olympiapublishers.com
OLYMPIA PAPERBACK EDITION

Copyright © Paul Devito 2024

The right of Paul Devito to be identified as author of
this work has been asserted in accordance with sections 77 and 78 of
the Copyright, Designs and Patents Act 1988.

All Rights Reserved

No reproduction, copy or transmission of this publication
may be made without written permission.
No paragraph of this publication may be reproduced,
copied or transmitted save with the written permission of the publisher,
or in accordance with the provisions
of the Copyright Act 1956 (as amended).

Any person who commits any unauthorized act in relation to
this publication may be liable to criminal
prosecution and civil claims for damage.

A CIP catalogue record for this title is
available from the British Library.

ISBN: 978-1-80439-429-8

This is a work of fiction.
Names, characters, places and incidents originate from the writer's
imagination. Any resemblance to actual persons, living or dead, is
purely coincidental.

First Published in 2024

Olympia Publishers
Tallis House
2 Tallis Street
London
EC4Y 0AB

Printed in Great Britain

Dedication

I dedicate this book to James Owens.

Chapter One

It was a cold winter night, and I was walking home from the coffee shop. We had had an ice storm the night before, and the ice still clung to the trees. The light from the streetlamps reflected off the ice, giving an eerie feeling to the neighborhood. There was a slight wind from the north, and my face was freezing. I trudged through the snow and ice, impatient to get home, which was only a couple of blocks from the coffee shop. I was still high from a joint I had smoked an hour earlier with friends of mine. I was thinking about Lisa, a college student, who lived only a few blocks away. She had long brown hair, green eyes, and a smile that would melt the ice off these trees.

I had just received a quarter of a million dollars from my mother, since she had inherited a million from her father. We had bought a two-family house in the university neighborhood, and my life had changed considerably. I had broken up with my old girlfriend and was a bachelor again. Since my money was in a trust fund that was invested very conservatively, I didn't have a very large income, but I didn't have to work, and I could concentrate on my writing. At that point, I had written four novels, and even though I had not been published, I had enjoyed some success from local friends who had read my work.

Finally, I arrived home. The snow in Syracuse, New York, can get pretty deep, and it can sometimes take a while to walk only a few blocks. I was tired, but I wanted to talk to Lisa since I hadn't seen her that day. The phone was busy the first time I called, and I wondered whom she could be talking to at nine o'clock. I rolled a joint, turned on the TV, and lay down on the couch.

I waited a few minutes; then I called her again.

"Hi, it's me," I said.

"What's up?" she said.

"Nothing, I guess. I just wanted to see what you were doing," I said.

"Actually, I'm writing a song," she said.

"Let me hear what you've got," I said.

She played the first part on her guitar and sang along with it. It was all right, but we all knew she wasn't going to make it as a songwriter or singer, even though she played in some local coffee shops. She was a very good sculptor and painter though and showed promise there.

"That's all I have so far," she said.

"Sounds good," I said.

"I'm going to change the chorus," she said.

"I think that's a good idea," I said.

"You always say everything's good. Then when I say I'm going to make changes, you say that's good too," she laughed.

"I'm very supportive of everything you do," I said.

I had known Lisa for about a year, and even though we spent a great deal of time together, we had never made love and were just best friends, though I wanted it to go further.

She was ten years younger than I was. I was thirty-three and had met her just before she had graduated from college. She was about five feet four and had a very sexy body. She didn't have the best sense of humor in the world, but she appreciated mine. We smoked pot together a lot and hung out, talking about whatever.

There was a group of us who hung out together. We were all interested in smoking pot, but that wasn't what kept us together. Little Mike was a guitar player, a good one, he was six-one, but we called him little because Big Mike was six-four. He waited on tables to make a living, but he always had his sights on making the big time in music. Big Mike was the golfer of the group and played golf with me a great deal. He was a salesman, but he always thought he could play on the tour. He could shoot even par every so often, but we didn't think he had the dedication to turn pro. Christina was Lisa's roommate and was twenty-three as well. She was blonde, blue-eyed, slender, and beautiful.

Harvard was also part of our group, though he was married and couldn't spend as much time with us as he would have liked. Harvard and Big Mike lived in Cortland, a small town south of Syracuse. I drove quite often to see them.

"What are you doing tomorrow?" I said to Lisa.

"I have to work in the morning, but I have the afternoon off," she said.

"Why don't you come over; we'll smoke some pot, listen to music, or you can paint," I said.

"Okay! About two?" she said.

"Good," I said.

I had a large, three-bedroom flat to myself, and late at night, it got pretty lonely. The pot made me feel comfortable. I was used to it, and it helped me relax and sleep. A few years down the road, it would become a problem but at this time, I was in the early stages of my addiction, and I still enjoyed it. I watched television for a couple of hours and then went to bed. I always went to bed early and got up early; I did my writing in the morning before I got stoned and then enjoyed the day. I could write poetry stoned but not novels.

The next day, Lisa came over, and the first thing I did was bring the bong out. With the bong, it felt more like a party and I treated her with my pot most of the time. I put some jazz on, and we sat back to relax. I always felt horny around her, but I never knew if she would ever fuck me or not. She always wore tight jeans, and every once in a while, I would let her catch me staring at her crotch. She liked to keep her legs spread, and I liked to stare.

"What's Little Mike up to?" she said.

"He might come over later; he has the day off," I said.

"I hope he brings his guitar," she said.

"What about Big Mike?" she continued.

"He's working. But I think I'll go down to Cortland tomorrow," I said.

It was difficult for me to bring our conversations to a deeper level. I wanted to tell her that I loved her, and even that I wanted to marry her, but I could never bring myself to say it. She had another part-time boyfriend named Jason at the time, and even though I knew it wasn't that serious, it troubled me. I didn't think he was good enough for her and, of course, I thought I was the better man, but there it was, and I was jealous. She spent a lot more time with me though, which I was happy about, and which gave me some sort of hope for the future.

"When was the last time you saw Jason?" I said.

"A couple of days ago."

"Did you fight again?" I questioned.

"Of course. Why should anything have changed?" she said.

"Why do you keep going out with him if you can't get along?" I said.

"I don't know. I like him."

I shook my head. She knew I was jealous, and she liked it. I looked out my bay window and noticed it was beginning to snow. It was dark and dreary in Syracuse for six months every year, and people got pretty bitchy after a while.

"It's snowing again," I said.

"It's only January, and I'm already sick of it," she said.

She sat back on the couch facing me and put one foot on the floor, spreading her legs. I looked right at her crotch, then looked away. I think she saw me.

"Jason's not right for you," I said.

"I know, but the sex is great," she said.

"Why have a relationship just based on sex?" I said.

"I like him too, but I wish he were more mature," she said.

"You should be fucking me," I said.

"We've been through this before."

"I'm sick of just being friends; you spend practically all your free time with me," I said.

"We're best friends. Can't you leave it at that?" she said.

"I guess I'll have to," I said.

I got up to make some coffee and offered her another bong hit. She refused. The snow was getting heavier, and I was thinking it would be good for cross-country skiing. Lisa and I often went skiing together. She was very athletic and loved the outdoors. I made the coffee and went back into the living room. Lisa was stretched out on the floor doing exercises. This drove me crazy. She spread her legs in those tight jeans and touched her toes. Then she grabbed her ankles and pulled her knees up to her head. I wanted to dive on her right there. She wanted me to watch her, so I did. Her ass was so tight and plump, I couldn't stand it. I took another hit.

"All right," I said, "that's enough of that; cut it out now."

"Okay," she laughed.

She sat back down, and I turned on the TV. There was nothing on, of course, so I put the music on again.

"Do you want to hear my latest poem?" I said.

"Sure."

I read the poem to her, and she said she liked it.

"I love the simplicity and consistency of your poems," she said.

"That's hard to achieve," I said.

"There's always a sensual, almost sexual, feel to your poems," she said.

"I'm a romantic," I said.

"So am I," she said.

I looked out at the snow and thought I would miss these simple times one day. I went into the kitchen and poured the coffee; I loved drinking coffee when I smoked pot.

"You're good with images of nature," she said.

"You might want to paint more from nature," I said, "but that's just a suggestion."

"Maybe we can go skiing this weekend," she said.

"I hope so," I said.

We talked for another hour or so, and then she decided to leave. I gave her a hug and kissed her goodbye on the cheek.

"Call me later," she said.

I watched that plump ass wiggle as she walked down the steps; then I went back into the living room to listen to Miles Davis.

Chapter Two

Later that day, Little Mike came over with his guitar.

As soon as he walked in, he said, "You've got to try this pot; it's phenomenal."

"Where did you get it?" I said.

"It's homegrown from up north," he said. "Look at it; it's purple and sticky as hell. Where's the bong?"

"Let me clean it out first," I said.

We sat down after I put fresh water in the bong and did a few hits. We were flying.

"Play some of your new work," I said.

"I wrote this last week; you'll like it," he said.

Transported by the pot, I listened carefully to his new song and enjoyed it immensely.

"That's great," I said.

"Yeah, I like it too," he said.

We sat and listened to Miles for a while. I had turned Mike on to Miles a few months earlier, and now he was hooked on him.

"How does he do that?" he said.

"It's magic," I said.

"Maybe it's the heroin or cocaine," Mike said.

The muted trumpet sounded like a wounded bird singing to its mate. That may not sound like a compliment, but to those who listen to him, they know what I mean. Mike followed along on his guitar, creating interesting riffs. He had a way of following and leading at the same time, which added flavor to the tune.

"Lisa came over earlier. She looked sexy as hell," I said.

"She always looks sexy," he said.

"I don't know why she won't fuck me," I said.

"The reason is, she knows that once she fucks you, she's gone," he said.

"I don't think that's true," I said.

"Of course it's true; the last three women you fucked, you said goodbye to," he said.

"Yeah, but I'm in love with Lisa."

"Sure you are."

I laughed. Mike had a way of putting things as though he always knew the truth about you, no matter how deluded you might be. He was dating a woman named Alicia, but they were on and off. They couldn't seem to stay together. He was like me, always looking for something better. I thought Lisa was great though, and had stopped looking, even if she was dating someone else.

"I am in love with her," I said, "or at least I think I am. What's the difference?"

"If you hit that for a while, you'd lose all interest," he said.

"Maybe, maybe not," I said. "I'd like to find out though."

"You need to start looking around; you can't rely on her," he said.

"I think you're right," I said. "When I was teaching at the university, I had tons of women. Now I don't have any."

"You might want to start teaching again," he said.

"Not yet," I said. "Hey, listen to this idea. I thought I would have a party for the gang and have everybody paint a picture on my back porch. What do you think of that?"

"That's a good idea," he said.

"I'm going to paint on the right-hand wall. I might do the

whole thing," I said.

"I can't paint to save my life," he said.

"Neither can I. What difference does it make back there?" I said.

I was interested and excited to start painting. I think it was Lisa's influence that gave me the idea. I didn't know at the time that my father's father had been a painter in Italy. It ran in my blood.

"I'll try it," he said.

"It'll be great," I said.

We hung out for a couple more hours. Then he went home. At least three inches of snow had accumulated; it was beautiful outside, with the flakes clinging to the trees and the streetlamps reflecting off them. That night, I went to bed early as usual and dreamed that I was a famous painter with beautiful women surrounding me, taking trips all over the world. When I was in Paris, I wore one of those painter caps and had a long, winding mustache. In Italy, I was the toast of the country, and they even had a ticker tape parade in downtown Rome. Then I woke up.

I usually felt good in the mornings. The pot didn't give me a hangover, so I always rationalized that it was better than alcohol. I put on a pot of coffee, lit a cigarette, and put a hit in the bong, my usual routine. I wasn't going to do any writing that morning. I was planning to go to the arts store and buy some materials for my painting party. I called Lisa and asked her to give me a list of all the things I would need.

She decided to go with me to pick out things herself while we were at the store. It didn't take very long. We were back at the house two hours later.

"What do you want to paint?" she asked as we got high on

the back porch.

"I don't know, but since I'm not good at drawing anything, I thought I'd do something abstract."

"That's a good idea," she said. "Just concentrate on your colors."

She was sitting very close to me, and I was tempted to kiss her, which I had never done before. She had her tight jeans on again; I couldn't help but take a peek at her crotch every once in a while. She had nice tits too, but she never wore anything low cut. Then I had an idea.

"Why don't you blow the smoke into my mouth after you take a hit?" I said.

"From a distance," she said.

She took a hit, and I got a few inches away from her lips as she blew the smoke into my mouth. As soon as she was finished, I kissed her. She looked at me in surprise. Then I tried to kiss her again. She pushed me away, and I pretended to pout.

"I told you from a distance," she laughed.

"Why don't you want to kiss me? I'm a very sexy kisser," I said.

"Don't start on me, Paul," she said.

"I bet I'm a better kisser than Jason," I said.

"We'll never know, will we?" she said.

"Never?" I said.

"Never say never," she said, "but let's get back to talking about painting."

"You were saying something about colors," I said.

"You might want to stick to the primary colors and work off them," she said.

"If I combine them, including white, I can come up with pretty much every kind of color, can't I?"

"That's right, and it'll teach you how to combine colors and how they work," she said.

"And just do any king of pattern?" I said.

"Just let it flow," she said.

"This will be interesting," I said.

"When are you going to start?" she said.

"Tomorrow morning."

Chapter Three

I woke up the next morning feeling good, and I prepared my materials the way Lisa had explained to me. I took a couple of hits of pot and got down to work.

The wall was already painted white. It was about six-feet wide and seven-feet tall. I took a two-inch-wide brush and dipped it into the blue paint. After mixing it with some white, I decided I would paint a space to look like water. It didn't really work, so I began mixing some other colors together and painting wide strokes across the wall. When I was finished with it, I was pretty excited. I called Lisa and asked her to come and look at it. She couldn't come over until the afternoon, so I was left alone with my creation for a few hours. Sometimes, when I looked at it, I really liked it; at other times, I didn't.

I took a long nap and woke up refreshed, curious to see how I would feel about it. With a new look at it, I decided it was okay, but I wanted to paint another wall. So much for the party and having everyone paint their own picture. Lisa arrived later that afternoon and was very supportive.

"There are some good things here," she said. "Your combinations of colors are very good. You have a feel for that, and like you said, your weakness is design, but that will come with time."

"I'm really excited about it," I said.

"You should be. If you keep working on it, you'll become a good painter one day," she said.

"I'm going to paint all the walls back here, and when I get better, I'm going to paint the living room wall," I said.

"You are excited!" she said.

We got high, and she left a couple of hours later after we talked a lot about famous painters. Little Mike came over later that evening, just to hang out. He was trying to put a band together and asked me for advice.

"I don't really know much about it," I said. "I guess there are musicians looking for work. You just have to find them."

"There aren't many good ones in this town," he said.

"Put the word out; I'm sure some will turn up," I said. "How's Alicia doing?"

"I went over there last night and fucked the living daylights out of her," he said. "That girl has a kinky side to her."

"Kinky, how?" I said.

"Last night, for example, she was on all fours, and I was fucking her from behind. Then just as I announced I was coming, she turned around, and I squirted my load right in her mouth!" he grinned.

"That's not kinky," I said.

"You don't think so?" he said.

"Now, if you were fucking her up the ass and she did that, it would be kinky!" I said.

He laughed so hard and took another hit on the bong.

"She won't take it up the ass," he laughed.

"What else does she like to do?" I said.

"She likes to lick my little bunghole," he grinned.

"That's a little kinky but still not anything spectacular," I said.

"She tied my hands to the bedpost one time," he said.

"That's nothing," I said. "She's just a normal gal looking for a little excitement."

"I guess so," he said.

"I put an ad in the newspaper for a roommate. I figured that's one way of getting a young girl around here," I said.

"Don't get one too young. You'll have all kinds of problems," he said.

"Yeah, you're right. I was thinking of a graduate student," I said.

"Perfect."

"It'll liven things up a little around here. It gets pretty lonely sometimes," I said.

"I understand," he said.

Even though I was lonely from time to time, I usually preferred living alone. I enjoyed having my own space and privacy. Then I would get sick of living alone and would search for a suitable roommate. Usually, the roommates were college students and would only last a few months.

"You know what you might want to do," I said. "You should put an ad for musicians up at the university. I bet there are a lot of talented people there."

"Yeah, I'm sure there are, but how long are they going to stick around?" he said.

"That's true," I said.

"Maybe there's an established band looking for a lead guitar player," I said.

"I haven't seen anything."

He stuck around for another hour, and then he went home to have dinner. I made a few phone calls after eating a sandwich and then turned on the TV. I usually didn't cook much for myself unless I felt like eating pasta. Sometimes, Lisa would come over and cook dinner for me; she was a good cook and always made something unique.

I went to bed and fell fast asleep. I woke up in the middle of the night, went out to the living room, and smoked a cigarette. I often did this, which was a terrible habit, but at that time, I couldn't break it. When I went back to bed, I had a beautiful dream about Lisa. It was more sensual than sexual. We were camping by a lake, as we had done in reality, and were lying naked by the water. She was posing for me in different positions, and I was simply admiring the view. She had such a beautiful body. We waded into the water and wrestled for a while, her bright eyes sparkling in the sunshine. I grabbed her ass playfully, and she pushed me away. Then I woke up. I realized how frustrated I was.

In the morning, I called her and woke her up. I usually got up before she did.

"Call me later," she said sleepily.

I did my routine, made the coffee, rolled a joint and smoked it while the coffee was brewing. In an hour, I was ready to paint again. Big Mike was coming up from Cortland to see me a couple of hours later, so I wanted to get right down to work. I prepared my materials and stared at the wall for a while before deciding what colors I wanted to use. I decided to try to create a forest effect and started with dark green. I mixed the blue and yellow and added a touch of dark red, but it quickly turned brown. I tried putting on just the green first and then adding the other colors, which worked.

I worked quickly, and after two hours, the wall was done. It looked better than the first wall, and I felt very satisfied.

Shortly after I finished, Big Mike showed up.

"Hey, big guy, what's up?" I said as he entered.

"Nothing much. How's the pot situation?" he said.

"I've got some," I said.

We went upstairs, and I cleaned the bong while he had a cup of coffee. He was a salesman and could pretty much make up his own schedule.

"What do you think of these?" I said, taking him to the back porch.

"Different," he said.

I knew that wasn't a compliment. We sat down on the couch on the porch and smoked some weed. He agreed with me that the second painting was better than the first.

"What got you interested in this?" he said.

"I don't know really; it just sort of happened, but I'm going to continue," I said.

"You've got a natural feel for colors," he said.

"Thanks."

"I can't wait to play some golf this spring," he said.

"Me too."

"What's going on with Lisa?" he asked.

"Same old thing. She won't fuck me."

"You've got to give her an ultimatum. Either she fucks you, or she's gone," he said.

"I've thought of that, but I can't do it. We've become such close friends," I said.

"It's just a ploy. You don't have to stick to it," he said.

"I know," I said, "but I can't do that to her."

"Do you want to fuck her?" he asked.

"Yes."

"Then do it," he said.

I thought about what Lisa's reaction to that approach would be, and I could imagine her ending our friendship. I didn't want to risk that, and I knew she wouldn't go for it. She had me right where she wanted me, and I was just along for the ride. It was beginning to snow, and the wind was blowing the flakes across my windows. It was very cold out that day, and I felt cozy on my little back porch.

"I'm not going to do it. I've already decided against it," I said.

"Then you'll never fuck her," he said.

"So be it. You can't get them all," I said. "What about your sex life?"

"I still see that girl Janice once a week, but I met someone the other day, and she gave me her phone number," he said.

"Where did you meet her?" I asked.

"At the pub down the street."

We smoked a little more, then went into the living room and turned on the TV. It was only background noise for us, and we talked for another hour or so until he had to leave. I called Lisa, but she wasn't home. I decided to get out of the house, and I walked to the coffee shop. It was freezing out, but I needed the exercise. My friend, Mark, was at the shop reading; he was a Ph.D. student and was always reading.

"What's up, buddy?" I said.

"Just hanging out a little," he said.

"What are you reading?" I asked.

"Philosophy and religion. What else?" he said.

"That stuff's bad for you," I laughed.

"No, it's bad for you," he said.

"I know. That's why I don't read it anymore."

I went to the counter and got a cappuccino. There were a few students doing homework, but I didn't know any of them. A beautiful young woman was sitting by herself, writing something. I decided I would approach her.

"What are you writing?" I said to her.
"A paper on Joyce," she said with a smile.
"*Ulysses*?" I asked.
"No, *A Portrait of the Artist as a Young Man*."
"I like that better anyways," I said.
"Are you familiar with Joyce?" she said.
"I taught English at the university," I said.
"Oh, an expert!" she exclaimed.
"Not on Joyce, I'm afraid," I said.
"What's your specialty?" she said.
"Theory," I said.
"Deconstruction?" she continued.
"I know a bit about it. I also studied philosophy in undergraduate school," I said.

I looked right into her eyes as we were talking, letting her know I was interested. She had blonde hair to her shoulders and blue eyes that glistened. She wasn't shy at all, so I asked her if I could sit with her for a minute.

"Of course. Sit down," she said.

I was trying to guess her age. She was about twenty-three or twenty-four. I figured she was a graduate student.

"Did you move to Syracuse to go to the university, or are you a native?" I asked.

"I'm a native," she said.

"Are you a graduate student in English?" I asked.

"No. I'm still an undergraduate student. I worked for several years before I went back to school," she said.

"Is this a course on just Joyce or a modern course?" I said.

"Modern," she said.

"Have you read any Virginia Woolf?" I said.

"*To the Lighthouse*," she said.

"That's my favorite," I said.

"I wasn't that crazy about it," she said.

"She's not for everybody," I said.

I wanted to get into a more personal conversation, but I was having trouble switching tracks.

"How do you like the university?" I said.

"I like it."

"I'm surprised you didn't want to go someplace else," I said.

"I was thinking of going to Boston, but I didn't get the courage to do it," she said.

"Are you tied down here in some other way? Boyfriend or something?" I said.

"No, not really."

That was the opening I was looking for.

"A beautiful girl like you doesn't have a boyfriend?" I said.

"Well, I had a boyfriend six months ago, but we broke up, or should I say I broke up with him," she said.

"What happened?" I said.

"He was very possessive and controlling. He's a great guy and everything, but he's immature."

"I understand. I lost a few women that way when I was younger."

I noticed she had started playing with her hair, which I took as a flirtatious action. She had me captivated by her smile. I was getting up the courage to ask her for her phone number, but I didn't know where to fit it in. I decided to end the conversation and ask her then.

"Listen, I have to go now, but I'd love to talk to you some more. Would you mind giving me your phone number?" I said.

"Not at all," she said.

She wrote down her number and gave it to me.

"What's a good time to call?' I asked.

"Any time after six," she said.

I was elated. I went home and thought about her for the rest of the evening. Her name was Linda, and I thought this friendship could develop into something more serious.

Chapter Four

The rest of that week, I painted three more walls and saw myself improving each time. I wanted to show Linda my most recent painting, which was a carousel on my living room wall. It turned out great, and I was beginning to think of myself as a painter. I called on her at the end of that week; she was studying and glad to have a little break.

"How did your paper turn out?" I said.

"I didn't get it back yet, but I wasn't happy with it," she said.

"Maybe you did better than you think."

"I hope so. What have you been up to?" she asked.

"I've been writing, and I've just begun to paint," I said.

"You're painting? How exciting!" she said.

"Yeah, it's great. I started a couple of weeks ago, and I am already improving."

"What medium?" she said.

"I'm using acrylics right now, but I think I want to switch to oils," I said.

"What are your subjects?" Linda asked.

"Well, I started with abstracts, but now I'm doing kind of blunt figures; I did a carousel on my living room wall that I would love for you to see."

"I'd like to see it."

"Why don't you come over tonight, and I'll cook you dinner," I said.

"That would be great," she said.

I gave her directions, and we agreed on six o'clock. I was excited and began to think about buying groceries. Big Mike called. I told him about Linda, and he proceeded to give me all kinds of advice on how to handle it.

"I suppose you're an expert," I said.

"I have a lot of experience; you have no idea what you're doing," he said.

"I have plenty of experience," I said. "Listen, I have to go buy groceries. I'll talk to you later."

What I was really thinking was whether or not I was going to try to kiss her on our first date, and where that might lead. I vacillated back and forth between trying to kiss her or not and really couldn't decide. I imagined making out with her on the couch, reaching down between her legs and everything else.

I went to get groceries; I bought steak and shrimp. I wanted to impress her. I also bought onions, potatoes and broccoli because I had nothing in my refrigerator. Then I spend the rest of the afternoon cleaning my place.

She was right on time, and I showed up at the door showered and freshly shaven. She was in a long, dark green coat, which I took for her as soon as we got upstairs. She saw the painting on the wall immediately.

"Wow, that's great!" she said.

"Thanks."

"You've only been painting two weeks and you did that? I'm impressed," she said.

"I still don't know how to paint figures or faces, but these turned out okay," I said.

I was glad she liked the painting. Then I took her to the back porch, where the madness began.

"You've made a lot of progress," she said.

"I have a long way to go, but I have a lot of ideas," I said.

"You're going to be great."

The evening was getting off to a good start, and I was thinking that I would be too afraid to kiss her. We sat in the living room. I put on some jazz and got us a bottle of wine. With the wine, I brought out the shrimp arranged neatly on a plate with cocktail sauce.

"You're quite the gourmet," she said.

"Not really."

I was sitting right next to her on the couch. She had sat in the middle, which seemed pretty strategic to me. Our faces were only a few inches apart, which was driving me crazy. I couldn't concentrate on what she was saying because I just wanted to kiss her. She ate a few shrimp and then stopped, while I kept right on eating. I didn't notice what I was doing, but pretty soon all the shrimp were gone.

"Oh, I'm sorry. I didn't realize I was eating so fast!"

"That's all right," she laughed.

"Do you like steak? I never asked you what you wanted to eat," I said.

"Steak is fine," she said.

Then I tried to kiss her.

She pulled away saying, "I don't kiss on the first date."

"Neither do I usually, but I can't resist you," I said.

I felt a little foolish, but I figured it wasn't a big deal.

"You can resist me," she said.

The wine tasted great, and our conversation went smoothly. We went from discussing literature to painting, history, and, finally, personal matters. I wanted to find out why she broke up with her boyfriend and what I could learn about her from that.

"He was temperamental," she said. "Every time I talked to

another guy, he would lose his temper. One time, he almost hit me."

"I'm not like that," I said. I'm very secure."

"That's what they all say," she said.

After a while, I decided to cook. Everything took only a few minutes, and I was satisfied with the final product. We sat at the dining room table. I noticed immediately that she was very dainty about the way she ate. I always ate very fast, so I tried to slow myself down.

"You're a good cook," she said.

"Sometimes, but I have a very limited menu," I said.

"What else do you cook?" she asked.

"I can cook pasta with several kinds of sauces. I went to Florence for a year when I was a senior at the university," I said.

We ate and talked. I really enjoyed her company. She was a good listener, and her conversation was interesting. She was soft-spoken but assertive enough in her opinions.

"Are you a Democrat or Republican?" I said.

"A Democrat mostly, but I have some Republican views, too," she said.

"You're liberal on abortion I take it."

"Yes," she said simply.

"Do you know much about monetary policy and the Federal Reserve?"

"No, not really," she said.

"I recommend you take a macroeconomics course," I said.

"I would hate that," she said.

"It's like spinach. It may not taste good, but it's good for you," I said.

"I'll eat broccoli," she laughed. "What about you?"

"I have opinions on both sides too, but mostly liberal," I said.

"Liberal on abortion?" she returned.

"Yes, but I'm not sure what I'd tell my own daughter or wife," I said.

"I suppose they would have to decide for themselves," she said.

"Yes, but I would be involved, too," I said.

"That's true," she said. "I got pregnant once."

"Did you have an abortion?" I asked.

"No, a miscarriage."

"What were you going to do?" I said.

"I was having a terrible time making up my mind, but I finally decided to keep it," she said.

"Was the father involved?" I questioned.

"No."

I was surprised she could talk about this on our first date, but I was impressed at the same time. She didn't seem at all ashamed of herself, nor should she have been. She was direct and proud.

"Why wasn't he involved?" I continued.

"Because we hadn't been going out for very long, and I had broken up with him before I found out I was pregnant," she said. "I consulted with my mother and father and decided to leave him out of it."

"Do you believe in God?" I said.

"No, not really," she said.

"Neither do I," I said.

"The miscarriage worked out well, I guess. I would have had a very difficult time going back to school with a child to take care of," she said.

"It can be done, but it's a lot harder, and it takes a lot more time," I said.

"I would have worked part time and gone to school part

time," she said.

"How do you swing it financially?" I said.

"My parents pay part, and I have grants and loans," she said.

I kept staring into her eyes. I wanted to kiss her in the worst way. After dinner, we sat in the living room, sipped wine, and talked some more. She liked my taste in music, and I was already imagining us married with children, living on the lake with mountains in the background. I tried to kiss her again. This time she let our lips meet for a few seconds. Then she pulled away.

"Stop now," she said.

"I'm sorry," I said.

"You don't have to apologize," she said, "but just be patient. You want this to last, don't you?"

"You're right," I said.

I liked that she had said that, because I did want it to last. I was not out to get laid. That didn't interest me. As we drank more wine, we began to laugh more. I was getting loose, and my sense of humor came out. I could see her eyes sparkle, and I was deeply infatuated.

"Are you taking any sports classes in the spring, like tennis or golf?" I said.

"I might take ballet," she said.

"I could teach you how to golf," I said.

"I would like that," she said.

"First, I would get behind you, put my arms around you, and show you the swing; it's important that you learn the grip and the hip movement," I said.

"I'm sure," she said.

"I'll teach you how to use my putter and my balls," I laughed.

"How many balls do you have?" she said.

"Right now, in my bag, a couple of dozen," I said.
"You're a freak!" she said.
"I'll use them all," I said.
"I only want to use two," she said.
"Let me know when you want to play," I said.
"Well, we'll have to wait until spring," she said.
"Noooo!" I laughed.

I poured her another glass of wine and thought about trying to kiss her again. She was getting pretty drunk, and I thought she might go for it this time. I noticed she touched my knee every once in a while. I just wanted to grab her. I resisted though, trying to be patient, knowing there would be other opportunities in the future. I wanted to smoke some pot, but I decided I would put that off, too.

"What do you like to do during the summer?" I said.

"I love being near the water, camping, fishing, swimming, you name it," she said.

"I was a swimmer in high school and a camp counselor during the summer for a few years. Once, a friend and I went over a waterfall in a canoe while the campers stood by watching in shock," I said.

"Did you get hurt?" she said.

"Neither of us had a scratch on us. The waterfall was only about ten feet high, and there weren't any rocks below it. We laughed for about five minutes after we got on shore safely," I said.

At that point, I leaned over and kissed her. This time she opened her mouth, and we slipped our tongues together, melting into a sensual kiss. I put my arms around her and pulled her close to me. After a few minutes, we separated.

"I told you not to do that," she said.

"I can't resist you," I smiled.

"I have to go anyway," she said. "I have a lot of studying to do."

"Can't we kiss a little more?" I said.

"We'll pick it up where we left off next time," she said.

Shortly after she left, I called Little Mike to tell him how it went. I was drunk, and I could hardly contain myself.

"You should see this woman, Mike. She's the most beautiful thing in the world!" I said.

"Whatever," he said.

He wouldn't be convinced, so I let it go and told him I would call him the next day. I smoked a bowl and took a hot bath. Then I went to bed, falling right to sleep.

Chapter Five

I woke up early, feeling a little hung over. I took some aspirin and went back to bed, but I couldn't fall asleep. I wanted to paint but didn't feel well enough to do it. I thought about Linda. Sweet images drifted through my mind. I was making love to her and enjoying tender moments in bed. I got up and made some coffee. Then I rolled a joint and felt a lot better after smoking it. A few minutes later, Lisa called to ask me what my schedule was for the day. I told her to come over that morning. I wanted to see her.

"What did you do last night?" she said.

"I had a hot date. I'll tell you about it when you get here," I said.

An hour later, she showed up wearing her tight jeans again. We smoked a bowl and talked.

"Her name is Linda. She's the most wonderful woman I've ever met," I said.

"Don't exaggerate," she said.

"She's beautiful, with a great body and a tight ass!" I laughed.

"You men are all alike," she said.

"I can't help it. I'm in love," I said.

"In love after the first date? How ridiculous!" she said.

"You're just jealous," I said.

"I'm not jealous," she said.

"You're not in love," I said.

"I know I'm not in love, but it'll come in time," she said.

"Why don't you fall in love with me?" I said.

"I love you," she said.

"Then why aren't you with me?" I said.

"I'm not in love with you," she said.

"I give up," I said.

"Good, now let's get back to Linda," she said.

I took another hit off the bowl and thought about Linda's beautiful face. I could tell by Lisa's questions that she was a little bit jealous, if not of Linda herself, then of what had begun between us.

"Does she smoke?" she said.

"Smoke what?" I said.

"Anything," Lisa said.

"I don't know if she smokes pot. We drank wine last night, but she doesn't smoke cigarettes," I said.

"Good! Is she smart?" she probed.

"Of course," I said.

"Is she religious?" she asked.

"No," I said.

"Good," she said. "Is she a student or working?"

"She's a student."

"Perfect! You can show off your knowledge," she said.

In my mind, I was comparing the two women, though I didn't know Linda well enough. I wanted to cause some trouble, so I grabbed Lisa and wrestled her to the carpet while she screamed and laughed at the same time.

"Cut it out!" she said.

"I'm only having fun!" I said.

"Come on, Paul, leave me alone," she said.

We stopped wrestling, and I kissed her quickly on the neck. She got back up on the couch and sat with her knees facing me.

"Did you grab Linda like that last night?" she said.

"I tried to kiss her a couple of times," I said.

"You guys have no patience. She's going to run if you're not careful," she said.

"I know, I know, but she's so beautiful I can't resist her," I said.

"Well, you'd better cool off. No woman wants to be obsessed over," she said.

"You're right, of course," I said.

"How old is she?" she asked.

"She's about twenty-four."

"That might work," she said, "but you should take it really slow."

"Yeah, now I wish I hadn't tried to kiss her," I said.

"That's all right. It shouldn't be a problem."

I wondered what Linda was thinking at that very moment. She was probably involved with school and wasn't thinking about me at all. On the other hand, perhaps the echo of the night before was ringing in her ears.

"I'm pretty sure she likes me," I said.

"I'm sure she does," Lisa said, "but you don't have to try to impress her. Just let her get into you. Listen, I have to go. I've got a lot of things to do today. I'll call you later."

"I'm thinking of going down to Cortland; if I'm not here, leave a message," I said.

After she left, I called Big Mike to see what he was doing.

"What's up, big guy?" I said.

"Nothing. Hey, listen. I'm all out of pot here. Have you got some?" he asked.

"Sure. Do you want me to buy you some quantity or just buy

you a little?" I said.

"Buy me an ounce, will you?" he said.

"Yeah, I'll be down in about an hour."

I stopped by my dealer's house and bought a couple of ounces. It was high quality, so I paid quite a bit for it. It was worth the extra money I saved in the long run. I rolled a joint in the car on the way down to Cortland and smoked it. Being high didn't affect my driving. I drove slower though and more cautiously. When I got there, Big Mike was smoking the little he had left.

"It's completely dry down here," he said. "By the way, how did your date go?"

"Excellently," I said. "She's great, really great."

"I'm a little worried about you," he said.

"Why?" I startled.

"You seem manic to me. You're not your usually relaxed self," he said.

"It's just that I'm excited about Linda, that's all," I said.

"I think you should talk to your doctor," he said.

"I will," I said.

We smoked some pot, and I thought no more about his warning. I could never tell when I was manic unless I began to lose sleep, which hadn't happened at that point. I took medication since I had had manic episodes before, and the pot worked to sedate me as well.

I told Mike about Linda, and he told me to take it slow, like Lisa had.

"If she's anything like you describe her, she's great," he said.

"I'm a little nervous," I said. "You know me. I fall head over heels and then something ruins it."

"Not always," he said. "You've had a couple of women ask you to marry them. Don't forget that."

"No. You're right. I've had my opportunities, but the ones I chase always get away," I said.

"Well then, stop chasing them. Play it cool," he said.

I was high as a kite and we started laughing about nothing. We talked about golf, and the goals we were setting for ourselves. He talked about playing on the tour, and I went along with it, thinking that if he really practiced, he would have a shot at it. I talked about painting, where I thought my style was heading, whom my influences were, and the newborn confidence I had.

When I left later that afternoon, I was exhausted. All I wanted to do was go home and sleep. I couldn't sleep at all though, as I kept thinking about Linda. That night was the first night I didn't take my medication. I forgot all about it. My mind was racing, and I was already too manic to notice my own symptoms.

The next morning, I got up, excited about the day. I smoked some pot and started painting right away. The phone rang several times, but I didn't answer it. My brush moved quickly. I was painting on a small canvas for the first time, and I was done in half an hour. It was a painting of Don Quixote, and I was really pleased with it. I called Lisa as soon as I cleaned up.

"Hey, what's going on?" she said.

"I did a great little painting," I said.

"What of?" she asked.

"It's a little man on horseback, a Don Quixote," I said, "with a wild sky behind him."

"Sounds cool. When can I see it?" she said.

"Anytime. I'll be here all day," I said.

"I'll be over about two," she said.

"Okay. See you later," I said.

I made some coffee and smoked more pot. I called Little Mike and talked to him for a few minutes. I told him about my new painting and about Linda, and he said he would try to stop over later in the day. Then I drank about five cups of coffee; I was flying by the time two o'clock rolled around.

Lisa looked great. She had her hair pulled back in a ponytail and was wearing a faded pair of jeans with a sweatshirt. I showed her the painting as soon as she walked in, and she was impressed.

"Hey, that's great!" she said. "You've come a long way in such a short time."

"Thanks. I'm glad you like it because you really know what you're looking at."

She could only stay for a short while, and I was kind of glad, because I had the urge to do another painting. I smoked more pot and sat down at my easel. In about twenty minutes, I finished a small painting, but I was not as happy with this one. I was very manic, and the combination of pot with coffee made it worse. The problem was that I only thought I was high, not manic. Whenever I got manic, I read philosophy, and this time was no exception. I picked up a book by Derrida and started the difficult task of trying to pull apart his arguments.

"Why," I thought, "would the signifier be disconnected from the signified?"

From there, I went into the wilderness of deconstruction, weaving and unweaving propositions. Being manic and philosophizing was very dangerous for me, but I was already too far gone to recognize it. My thoughts were racing, and they took me right out my front door. It was late afternoon, and it was already starting to get dark. The wind was blowing and I was only wearing a sweater. I wasn't conscious of where I was going, but I ended up heading toward the university. I walked quickly, trying to keep my body warm, as if I were going some place in particular. For hours I walked, deep into the middle of the night, solving problems that probably didn't even exist.

I walked around and around the campus, not talking to anyone but myself and ended up by the sorority houses. There I found an empty house; apparently, they were doing some construction work on it. I entered it through the back door and found their secret meeting room in the basement, which amazed me. There were all kinds of strange things for their rituals: hoods, candles, masks, and symbols on the walls.

"How does a symbol signify?" I asked myself.

"It reverberates, spreading other meanings and feelings in different directions," I answered myself.

I went upstairs to the kitchen and looked in the refrigerator. It was empty. A woman upstairs had heard me and came into the kitchen, startling me.

"Who are you?" she said.

"Paul. I'm a member of this sorority," I said.

Then a man walked in. He was her husband.

"What are you doing here?" he said.

"I came in to get warmed up," I said.

They spoke to each other quietly; I couldn't hear them. Then he left the kitchen.

"Can I get you a glass of orange juice?" she said.

"Sure."

A few minutes later, two policemen walked in.

"What's your name?" one said.

"Paul," I said.

"Full name? Do you have any I.D.?" he said.

"Paul Devito," I said, giving him my driver's license.

"What are you doing here?" he said.

"Thinking," I said.

"Come with us," he said.

They put me in the police car and drove me to the local jail. They fingerprinted me and took my picture. They walked me through the jail and put me in a cell. I thought I was getting ready to meet some important dignitary or something; I didn't know what was happening to me. I felt the wind rushing through my ears and thought the rain was pelting against me.

After a while, realizing that nobody was coming to meet me, I took my prison clothes off in protest and stuffed my mattress out of the food slot. The guards didn't like that too much and started giving me shit.

"Cut that out, Paul, or we'll tear your head off," one said.

I quieted down, but I could still feel the wind and the rain beating against my body. My mind was somewhere else. I was in a world of words, phrases, sentences, and arguments.

"The signifier triggers a response, a chemical response that travels throughout the mind and body, not just other signifiers," I said to myself. "But every signifier is different for the same signifier," I added, "and every signifier is different from itself."

I didn't sleep at all again that night, and I didn't want anybody else to sleep either, so I kept whistling as loud as I could, all night long.

"Cut that out," the guy in the neighboring cell said every once in a while.

The next morning, they took me in front of the judge, who immediately ordered the guards to take me to the hospital. By then, I had regained my senses a little bit but needed hospitalization desperately. On the way over to the hospital, I spoke harshly to the guards, returning the favor they gave me the night before. When I got to the hospital, they gave me a complete examination, and then I took a nice hot bath. After they gave me the medication, I fell right to sleep and slept for sixteen hours.

When I awakened, I knew right where I was and what had happened. I called my mother to tell her where I was, and she came in the afternoon to visit me.

"How are you feeling?" she said.

"Not bad considering. As soon as I got some sleep, I came back to my senses," I said. "I have to be here for a few weeks for my medication to stabilize."

I told her about my jail story and how the guards had roughed me up, thinking that I was faking my illness.

"They're brutes," she said. "I told you several years ago about that trial against the guards when I was on the jury. They just killed a man for no reason."

She always made me feel better. I felt refreshed after her visit. She told me she would be back the next day. I called my brother and talked to him for a while. He made me feel better too. I had been in the hospital a couple of times before and knew the routine well. I hadn't been hospitalized for five years and discovered that I didn't know any of the nurses. The aides were new as well, so I spent the next few days getting to know the staff.

I was unique in the hospital. After my medication kicked in, I was sane. I was well educated, and I could function at a high level. The other patients were much sicker than I was and could not function at all. I spent all my time hanging out with the nurses and aides, and most of the time, I was bored to death. When I felt stronger, a few days later, I called Little Mike.

"Hey, what's going on?" I said.

"Where have you been? I've called a million times and left

messages. You were nowhere to be found," he said.

"I had a breakdown. I'm in the hospital right now."

"What time are visiting hours? I'll be there this afternoon," he said.

I felt great after talking to him. He would bring some excitement into the hospital.

One of the aides on the day shift was named Heather, and I liked her immediately. She had brown hair and eyes, and a beautiful smile. She also had dimples, which I had a weakness for. She liked me too, possibly because I was the only patient she could really talk to. She liked to play cards, so we played gin and talked. Heather was a couple of years younger than I was, and she didn't have a boyfriend.

"I called my friend, Mike. He said he'd visit me this afternoon," I said to Heather.

"Good! It's nice to have company in here. So few of the patients get visitors," she said.

"He's a kick, a great guitarist with a tremendous sense of humor," I said.

"He'll liven things up around here then," she said.

I watched her face closely as she studied her hand and selected a card. I imagined kissing her and sneaking into the bathroom to make love to her. Then I thought about Linda. I wondered if I should call her and tell her what had happened. I told Heather about Linda, and she suggested that I wait until I got home before I called her. I wanted to go home in the worst way, but I knew I just had to sit there for a few weeks.

"What kind of books do you read?" I asked Heather.

"Mysteries and thrillers," she said. "What about you?"

"I like the classics and some contemporary autobiography," I said.

"What do you write?" she said.

"Fiction and autobiography."

"I'd like to read one of your books sometime," she said.

"No problem," I said.

"Is there any sex in them?" she said.

"Sure," I said.

"Wild sex?" she said.

"Not really," I laughed.

She had such great facial expressions, some of them very subtle. I tried to make her laugh so I could see her dimples. After playing cards, I took a nap. The meds they had me on were pretty strong, so I slept quite a bit. When I got up, it was lunchtime. The food was decent and since there wasn't anything else to do, I ate voraciously.

Later that afternoon, Little Mike showed up. I felt better just seeing him.

"How's the cuckoo's nest?" he said.

"Lovely," I said.

"You should start a revolution and free all the nuts," he laughed.

"I'm simply trying to get out of here myself," I said.

"Some of the nurses in here are hot," he said.

"Come on. I want to introduce you to somebody," I said.

Heather was sitting in the living room, reading quietly. I brought Mike over and introduced them.

"Keep an eye on this guy. He's my buddy," Mike said.

"He's keeping an eye on me," she said.

"That's all right too," he said.

"Heather plays the piano," I said.

"What kind of music do you play?" Mike said.

"Classical and jazz," she said.

"Very nice," he said.

"What about you?" she said. "I hear you play the guitar."

"Yeah, I play mostly rock. I write my own stuff," he said.

"I wish I could write," she said.

"It's not as hard as you think," he said. "You should try a little every day. It'll start to come to you."

Heather brushed her hair back with her hand and smiled. She really looked beautiful at that moment. I wished, when I looked at her, that we had met under different circumstances. Mike and I left Heather alone and went to my room to talk.

"So, what happened to you?" he said. "I don't know anything about these nervous breakdowns."

"They're all different," I said. "My problem is that when I go off my medication, I get manic or high and go off the deep end."

"Yeah, but what does that mean?" he asked.

"For me, it means that my mind races and I don't get any sleep until finally, I stop making sense when I talk," I said. "It's kind of like going into a dream state when you're awake."

"That's all right. I never make sense when I talk," he laughed.

"This is a little different," I said.

He was getting uneasy about being in the hospital. Even though we were in my room, we could hear the craziness around us. He left and told me he would be back again soon, possibly with Lisa. I hung out in the living room with Heather until dinner, and I ate two platefuls of food again.

The hospital was downtown, and at night there was a great view of the city lights. I watched the cars drive by on the streets below and felt relieved that at least I was in a safe place. It was a windy night, but it wasn't morning, so there was a clear view across the city. I watched the trees wave in the wind. They spoke to me of different times and different places. I thought about Laura, an affair I had had when I was younger. Where was she now and with whom? I thought about something de Man had written. As a pessimist, he noted that time is passing. Yes, time is passing, and it is painful. But what would there be without motion?

He noted there is no knowledge, but what of it? I know God doesn't exist. How do I know that? How can I read that sentence? I was still manic, as these thoughts of philosophy still ran around in my head. I tried to ignore these thoughts and think about the women I had known in my life.

Suddenly, it began to snow. The wind whipped the flakes against the window, and the lights below began to blur. I went to my room and got my Walkman. I listened to some soul and went back to the window. Time took on a different dimension in the hospital. It didn't move. I thought about Nietzsche and how he was probably manic-depressive. He knew the lows of depression, which he associated with pessimism, and he knew the highs, which became his famous optimism. I am an optimist, not by choice, but by nature.

The music made me feel good. It took me away. Laura, Lisa, Linda, all versions of women, are different, but all the same too. They were my inspiration. I used nature but took inspiration from the women. They were beautiful, so graceful. I loved to watch their hands hold a teacup, smoke a cigarette, and flick their hair back. I loved to make their eyes lively and make them smile and laugh.

I went back to the lounge and asked Rita, the night aide, if she wanted to play cards. She agreed and dealt a hand of gin. She was not beautiful, but she had a kind heart and was a good conversationalist.

"You seem deep in thought, Paul," Rita said.

"Yeah, I need to lighten up a little," I said.

"Heather says you're a writer and a painter."

"I've been writing for a long time, but I just started painting."

"That's great! And you were also a teacher?" she said.

"Yeah, but I gave that up when I got sick at one point," I said.

"You've got to take better care of yourself," she said.

"I know."

I had a joint in my pocket that Little Mike had brought me. I wanted to go into the bathroom to smoke it. I knew that would help ease my thoughts. After the card game, I told Rita I wanted to take a shower and went to my room to get my pajamas. I took my shower and smoked the joint, which made me feel a bit better. I was addicted and had been going through a light withdrawal.

I stayed up for a couple of hours, enjoying my high, and then went to bed. I slept well and felt great in the morning.

Chapter Six

The days passed slowly, and I was bored to death. The only breaks from the boredom were the art classes they gave. I worked on sketching faces, which I knew nothing about, and eventually got pretty good at it. I had Heather pose for me, and when one turned out really well, she was thrilled.

"This is so great, Paul. You're getting good at this," she said.

"Thanks."

I had captured the sparkle in her eyes and her gentle expression. I wanted to kiss her in the worst way, but I didn't know how she felt about me. I wanted to catch her alone one day so that I could talk intimately to her, and that day came soon.

We were playing cards about a week into my stay when the day room was empty except for us. I didn't know how to tell her that I liked her, but I knew I had to build up to it. At one point, we were talking about Lisa and how we had managed to be just friends for years.

"I admire that in you," Heather said.

"I see no point in breaking up a great friendship just because someone doesn't want to have sex," I said.

"Most men are not like that. They want everything or nothing, and that's why their relationships don't last."

"She really cares about me, and I'm willing to settle for that," I said.

"I have a friend like that," she said.

"Does he want to sleep with you?" I asked.

"Yes, but he doesn't ask anymore."

"I still ask once in a while," I said.

"She might give in one day. You never know," she said.

"I'm not worried about it."

Heather's hands were so delicate. I watched her pick up and put down cards as if she were massaging my body. I decided I would go for it.

"I really like you, Heather."

"I like you too, Paul."

"Enough to kiss me?" I said.

"It's not very professional, but I've thought about it," she said.

"Have you ever dated an ex-patient?" I said.

"No."

"I was thinking maybe we could go out to dinner after I get out," I said.

"We'll see," she said.

I let it go at that. It wasn't a no, but it wasn't a yes, either. My advances didn't affect the way we related to each other. We continued to play cards and just changed the subject. At least I had another friend, but I really wanted to make love to her. That night I fantasized about her and dreamt sweet dreams.

The next morning, I woke up early, which was my normal habit, so I knew I was almost well again. The night nurse was still up. I talked to her for several hours and enjoyed a long hot shower. I ate a big breakfast and waited patiently for Heather to arrive. I took my medication and was told I had an appointment with my doctor that day. As I was going to my room, a female patient ran down the hallway naked with an aide chasing her. He grabbed her and led her back to her room. She smiled at me as she passed.

It was the best laugh I had had so far. Heather arrived at eight. I was clean-shaven and dressed in new clothes, which made me feel better.

"You look sharp," she said.

"Thanks, you look nice too."

"Are you going to sketch me today?" she asked.

"Sure."

She had some work to do, so I went into the living room to read and smoke. I wanted to go to the coffee shop and hang out with my friends. After a while, I took out my sketchpad and tried to draw my own face by looking into the mirror. It didn't work. Heather was done with her chores a little later.

After she had finished her work, we got together and she posed for me again. This time the sketch was magical. There was a hint of idealization in it, which made her look even more beautiful than she was. She loved it.

"I want to see your paintings after you get out," she said.

"That would be great," I said.

"Do you think you could do a painting of me?" she asked.

"I don't know. I could try."

We played cards until my mother came to visit. It was a short visit. She was pleased with my progress and wasn't worried about me. Later on, I was expecting Lisa, who had told me she was going to bring me a bag of pot. I really wanted to get high, just to make my stay more tolerable.

I ate a big lunch, and an hour later, Lisa showed up.

"I've never been in a psychiatric hospital before," she said. "It's a little spooky."

"The first time is always uncomfortable, and every time after that too," I said. "You don't have to stay long."

"When are you getting out?"

"A few more days," I said. "Hey, I want to show you the sketches I've done in here."

I pulled out my sketchbook, and she went through it slowly from start to finish.

"You've really improved," she said.

"Yeah, I'm getting the hang of it."

She left a little while later, which gave me the opportunity to smoke some pot. I escaped into my own world and sketched the scenery from the window. I think Heather knew I was high, but she didn't say anything. I felt like I was back to my normal self, and it was only a matter of time before they opened the doors.

Chapter Seven

Four days later, I was out. I can't explain how exhilarating it was to be free after being locked up. My apartment was the way I had left it. My mother helped me clean it, and she brought my cat. My feline had really missed me. Our reunion was quite touching. I called all my friends and told them I was out. We planned a dinner party for that Friday night, which was two days away. I told Little Mike that I had some pot. He decided to come over that evening. I got some sleep and then did some writing. Little Mike showed up around dinnertime.

"Hey, how does it feel to be out?" he said.

"Great, of course," I said.

We smoked a little from the bong, and he played the guitar. I was so grateful to be home and have close friends.

"Did you fuck that nurse you liked?" he said.

"No, but she did give me her phone number. I'm going to call her in a few days. She's sweet, isn't she?" I said.

"She seemed nice. I didn't really get a chance to talk to her."

"I can talk to her about personal things. I told her all about myself, and she didn't bat an eye."

"Sounds pretty serious."

"I don't know. I'm also infatuated with Linda. She's so beautiful," I said.

"You're like me. You go from woman to woman, thinking every time that this is the one, but it never works out," he said.

"They don't have the sense of humor I'm looking for," I said.

"Most women don't have a great sense of humor," he said.

"Then I'll stay single," I said.

"We'll probably both stay single," he said. "On top of that, they don't appreciate art enough."

I made some spaghetti, and we ate a ton of food. I could make a good sauce. I put olive oil, garlic, onions, and meat with plum tomatoes in a pan and cooked it quickly. I didn't have the patience to wait all day. There was always something special about breaking bread with Mike. We shared the eye of the artist, the pain and suffering of trying to create something great and, of course, the frustration of failure. They don't understand, we kept saying. They know only the banality of mediocrity. This is what all artists always say. But does it help?

"What's going on with you and Alicia?" I said.

"I think I'm going to break up with her."

"Why?" I asked.

"Same old reason. She doesn't understand me or appreciate me."

"Keep looking," I said.

After eating, Mike picked up the guitar again, and we sang some songs. We smoked more pot, and it felt like we were on top of the world. He left a couple of hours later, and I went to bed early as usual. It was lonely in my apartment, but I didn't care. I had all the space to myself and could work in peace.

Two days later was the dinner party. I had invited Lisa, Heather, Big Mike, Little Mike, Harvard, and Christina. I went shopping and bought all kinds of food. Besides spaghetti, we were going to have breaded veal cutlets, broccoli, mashed potatoes, and ice cream. Lisa went shopping with me and helped prepare the food. Little Mike came over early and played the guitar while we worked.

"I hope we have enough food," I said.

"We've got tons of food," Lisa said.

"I know, but everyone is going to have the munchies," I said.

I loved to watch Lisa work. Her ass wiggled as she whipped the potatoes. I was worried that Heather might feel uncomfortable since she didn't know anyone. Everybody showed up at six o'clock, and we sat on the couches and chairs in the living room. I didn't know if Heather smoked pot, but I figured she wouldn't care if we did. I had cleaned the bong and had bought a beautiful bag of pot.

"Where'd you get this?" Big Mike said about the pot.

"My usual source, but he got a special shipment in," I said.

"Would you like to smoke a little?" I said to Heather.

"Sure," she said.

I was relieved. It probably wouldn't have made a big difference if she hadn't smoked, but this way I knew she wouldn't give me shit about it. We started getting pretty silly after smoking. The conversation was not exactly esoteric.

"Play something, Mike," I said, "and you sing along, Lisa."

"I'll sing too," Big Mike said.

"Forget it then," I said. "No, you two go ahead."

"I don't want to play now," Little Mike said. "You have to cook anyway."

"Hey, did you see the new clerk at the bookstore?" Christina said.

Everybody said no.

"It's a he-she or a she-he. I don't know which," she said.

"Well, was he a man first who became a woman, or the other way around?" Harvard said.

"She was a man first," Chris said.

"Then it's a he-she," Big Mike said.

"Isn't that a little derogatory," Lisa said.

"Of course, it is," Harvard said. "She's just a she now."

"Why would they hire her?" Big Mike said.

Probably because she knows a lot about books," Lisa said.

"Okay, enough about he-shes. Obviously, Lisa is getting offended," I said.

I went to the kitchen to cook the food while the others sat around, talking and laughing. Lisa came in a few minutes later to help out.

"I like Heather. She seems nice," Lisa said.

"Yeah, I can really talk to her," I said.

"I don't think she usually smokes pot," she said.

"I don't think so either," I said.

The pasta was ready after a short while. We gathered around the dining room table, sitting down in a random order. I served everybody, and there was no conversation for a while, since everybody was stuffing their faces. Finally, Heather spoke up.

"Paul did some great sketches in the hospital. You should show everybody, Paul," she said.

"I will," I said.

"His paintings have improved dramatically," Lisa said.

"I love the painting on the living room wall," Heather said. "What do you call your style?"

"I've been thinking about it. Maybe 'illusionism' says it best."

"That's a good name," Little Mike said.

"You write like you paint," Big Mike said.

"Do you really think so?" I said.

"*The Masqk* is illusionistic," he said.

"Yes, but that's different from everything else I've written," I said.

The food was delicious. After the pasta, I went back to the kitchen to cook the veal cutlets. I was glad Heather liked my work, but I was afraid to give her one of my novels. They were a bit too personal. Most people don't understand that even in an autobiography there is a great deal of fiction. I always exaggerated the truth and invented stores to make my novels more interesting.

After eating the cutlets, mashed potatoes, and ice cream, we all sat in the living room again and smoked more pot. I'm sure Heather was surprised at how much pot we smoked, but I figured she might as well know what she was getting into. I asked her to stay after the others left, and she agreed.

"I like your friends," she said.

"They're great," I said. "How do you feel?"

"I'm pretty high," she laughed. "Do you smoke every day or just on occasions like this?"

"Pretty much every day," I said. "How about you?"

"Just occasionally."

I was looking directly into her eyes. I wanted to make love to her but knew I should move cautiously. She seemed very playful, touching me and laughing like a little girl. As I was sitting next to her, my hand slipped around her shoulders, and I kissed her. She kissed me back.

"I like you, Heather."

"I like you too."

I kissed her again, and our tongues played with each other. I reached down to play with her breast, but she pushed my hand away. We kissed some more, and I moved my body on top of hers. She started moaning as I separated her legs and thrust up against her. She arched her back and pushed her tongue deep into my mouth. I put her hand in my pants, and she felt my throbbing cock.

"That feels so good," I said.

"You're quite big," she said.

"You really excite me," I said.

I unzipped my pants and pulled out my cock. She massaged it slowly as I slipped my hand under her pants. She was so wet. I put two fingers inside her, and she moaned again. I rubbed her clitoris, and she came a minute later.

"Let's make love," I said.

"Do you want to put it in my mouth?" she said.

"Yes."

I pulled down my pants and climbed up on her. She opened her mouth and stuck her tongue out slightly. I slipped it in, and it felt so good. She was talented. It wasn't long before I came in her mouth. She swallowed it and smiled afterward.

"You taste good," she said.

"It felt great," I said.

"Let's save the fucking for next time," she said.

"Okay."

We took a shower together, and she rubbed my cock with her soapy hand. I felt like telling her that I loved her, but I knew it was too soon. I knelt down in the shower and licked her pussy. The water streamed down my face. I couldn't taste her juices. Afterward, I asked her if she wanted to spend the night, but she declined. I kissed her goodnight and took a hot bath to relax. I smoked a joint as I took my bath and thought I was in love. As usual, I imagined being married to Heather, what it would be like to have children with her, where we would live, etc.

Then I thought I should call Linda, who was more beautiful than Heather, and whom I could talk to about literature. I decided to call Linda the next day when I was sober. I slept well, being very drowsy from the pot. In the morning, I did my writing as usual and thought about what kind of painting I would do next.

Chapter Eight

I went to the coffee shop to see who was hanging out. Mark was there as usual, studying. I sat with him for a few minutes.
"Any major breakthroughs?" I said.
"Just the same old garbage," he said.
"I thought you liked reading that stuff," I said.
"Some of it," he said. "But a lot of it is ridiculous."
Just then, Linda walked in with her knapsack. She looked great. Her hair was pulled back in a ponytail, and she was wearing a large, dark green parka.
"Hi," I said.
"I was hoping to run into you," she said.
"Cold out there," I said.
"Unbelievable," she said. "Can I join you guys?"
"Sure."
She went to order a cappuccino and a muffin and Mark raised his eyebrows in approval.
"Wow!" he said. "Where'd you meet her?"
"Right here."
When she came back, I introduced her to Mark. I could tell he was a little nervous. Linda had a presence about her. She carried herself like a queen, and the men groveled in her wake. I was quite a bit older, so I could keep my cool, but I was a bit nervous too.
"I haven't seen you in a while. Where have you been hiding?" she asked me.

"I've been doing a lot of painting," I said.

I wanted to tell her about my breakdown but thought I should wait until I got to know her better.

"Do you think you could paint me sometime?" she said.

"I can try. I'm still a beginner," I said. "Do you want to pose naked?"

"Maybe," she said.

"I'm just kidding. I'll do your face," I said.

Then I thought about Heather and felt like I was hiding something. Now I had to choose between them, and I couldn't. I wanted them both, but knew it was ridiculous.

"What are you studying, Mark?" she asked.

"Philosophy."

"Oh, I hate that," she said.

"I don't blame you," he laughed.

"Would you like to come over for lunch and let me do some sketches of you?" I asked Linda.

"I can't today. I've got class, but maybe tomorrow," she said. "I've got to go now. Give me a call."

"I will," I said.

I couldn't get over how gorgeous she was as I watched her leave.

"You're lucky," Mark said.

"Not yet," I said.

"You've got that artist rap going on. She'll definitely come over to your place," he said.

"But I want her to fall in love with me. That's a different thing altogether, plus there's somebody else in the picture," I said.

"You've got another girlfriend?" he asked.

"Yeah, it looks that way. Listen, I've got to go. I've been

thinking about a painting I want to do, and it can't wait," I said.

"Let me know what happens," he said.

It was bitterly cold outside, and the wind was directly in my face. When I got home, I had to thaw out for a while before I could start moving. I smoked a joint and felt better instantly. Then I took out a new canvas and set up my paints. I had decided to paint a Don Quixote, with the horse walking through a stream. It turned out very well. I was happy with it, and because I had done it in acrylic, it dried quickly. I wanted to show it to Lisa, so I gave her a call.

"How did it turn out with Heather last night?" she said.

"We ended up in bed."

"Wow! That was fast. Now the hard work begins," she said.

"I know. I also saw Linda today, so I'm really confused. Do you want to come over and see this new painting?" I asked.

"Sure."

An hour later, Lisa showed up. She was wearing her tight jeans, and her hair was down.

"How did you persuade Heather to sleep with you on the first night?" she said.

"Well, I really think it was the pot, and she's pretty confident about herself. She's not worried that it was a one-night stand."

"Are you sure you did the right thing?" she questioned.

"Not really," I said.

"You never know how she's going to react to it today," she said.

"I hope she doesn't flip out," I said.

I brought the painting out and Lisa was really impressed.

"This is the best one you've done so far."

"I think so too."

"You've developed a style now that nobody else has. That's

a great achievement," she said.

"I'm teaching myself a lot of new things. I think it helps not having had any instruction," I said.

"You really have a natural feel for color," she said.

We smoked some pot, and I brought out my guitar for her to play. She was so sexy when she sang. I felt like grabbing her. She had to teach a little while later, but we thought we could get together that evening. After she left, I called Little Mike.

"Hey, what's up?" he said.

"I've got a new painting, and I'm very happy with it."

"Great, why don't I come over in a couple of hours?" he replied.

"Sure. I also fucked Heather last night."

"You did? On the first date?" he said.

"Yeah, she was pretty fucked up. I don't know how she'll feel about it today," I said.

"How was she?" he said.

"She tasted great. She's a good fuck."

After I got off the phone, I thought about Linda and Heather; I didn't know what to do. I figured I could go out with both of them for a while until I knew how I felt. As I looked out the bay window, I noticed it was beginning to snow. The winter drags on endlessly in Syracuse. One has to fight off the blues. My cat perched herself on the windowsill and stared at the street below, watching the other cats walking around.

I had a great feeling of accomplishment after a painting that I liked, and I was thrilled that Lisa appreciated it. This Don Quixote was the kind of painting that most people would like, I realized, and that was exactly what Little Mike said.

"This is a good one," he said. "This will be hanging in a museum one day."

"Stop teasing me."

"No. It's really good."

"Lisa liked it too."

"You've got a better sense of design now," he said.

"I can't wait to show it to Heather," I said.

"Have you talked to her today?" he asked.

"Not yet."

I was afraid to call Heather because I didn't know what kind of reaction she would have to the exploits of the night before. Mike thought she would be okay with it, but I wasn't too sure.

"I saw Linda this morning too. I don't know which one I want to go out with," I said.

"You may not have a choice, depending on how Heather reacts to last night," he said. "Couldn't you restrain yourself?"

"Once I start kissing a girl, I keep going until she says no; Heather didn't say no," I said.

"Call her up. Let's see what she says."

"I'm not going to call her with you here."

"Why not? What difference does it make?" he said.

"How can I talk to her intimately with you listening?" I reasoned.

"I'll go to the back porch and smoke a joint while you talk to her."

"Okay, let's do that."

I was nervous as I dialed the number; I didn't want her to yell at me. She was home and had a very pleasant voice as she said hello.

"Hi. It's Paul."

"Hi, sweetheart. What are you up to?" she asked.

I was so relieved that I felt elated.

"Nothing. I just wanted to talk to you. Listen, I'm sorry I was all over you last night. That's usually not my style. I…"

"It's all right. I didn't do anything I didn't want to do."
"Are you sure it's okay?" I said.
"Sure."
"Next time we won't get high, and we'll just talk."
"That's no fun," she said.
"Well, I don't want you to think that all I'm interested in is sex."
"I don't think that."

She was so sweet and understanding, I could hardly believe it. I knew that when a relationship starts that fast, it usually burns out just as quickly, so I wanted to slow it down, and I told her so. She agreed, and we let it go at that. We planned on getting together the next day; I told her about the painting, and she was excited to see it.

I went to the back porch and told Mike what had transpired. He was happy for me and teased me about being a bullshitter. We got the bong out and did a few hits. I grabbed the guitar and listened to him play. While he played, I thought about Linda and Heather. Even though I knew I should stick to the one I already had, I liked the chase, and Linda was a challenge. Mike left several hours later. I spent the evening alone with my own thoughts.

In the morning, I woke up feeling good, made my coffee and sat down to write. I wrote a poem about a man and his garden of birds. One bird in particular, a cardinal, left the garden and didn't return for three days. When she returned, she was exhausted and promised never to stray again. He fed her on the windowsill and let her listen to his music. It turned out pretty well. I was happy with it and decided to make it a series.

Chapter Nine

I smoked a joint and went to the coffee shop. I was hoping to run into Linda. Mark was there, so I sat with him. Usually, people couldn't tell that I was high, but Mark always knew.

"You're high, aren't you?" he said.

"Yeah."

"You'd better stop smoking that stuff."

"I'll quit one day."

"I'm sure you will, but if you want to go back to teaching, you'll have to quit soon."

"I don't know that I want to go back to teaching."

"Don't you feel that, without a job, you've lost direction?" he asked.

"What's so great about direction? All artists are directed by their work. They don't need a structure superimposed on them," I said.

Just then, Linda walked in.

"Hi," she said. Didn't I see you guys here yesterday?"

"That's us," I said.

She looked great as usual, but this time her hair wasn't pulled back. It was down, and she looked sexier than hell. Then I remembered we were thinking of getting together that day, but I had already promised Heather.

"Studying philosophy again, Mark?" she said.

"As usual," he said.

"My philosophy is to avoid studying anything painful," she

said.

"He actually likes it," I said.

"You like it too. You majored in it," Mark said to me.

"That's true. I confess."

"Are we getting together today?" Linda asked me.

"I can't today," I said. "My friend, Mike, was planning to come over. We're going to jam for a while."

"You play an instrument?" she asked.

"I play a little keyboard," I said.

I felt uncomfortable lying to her, so I made up some excuse and went home. It was snowing outside, and the wind was blowing. I put my hood up, but the wind penetrated anyway, and my ears froze. As I walked, I thought about how rude I had been and wondered if Linda was angry with me. I knew that trying to date two women wouldn't work. I had to choose one, and it had to be soon. When I arrived home, I called Heather, but she didn't answer. It was Sunday; I figured she was still sleeping.

I called Lisa, who got up early, even on Sundays, and she was home.

"Hey," I said.

"What's up?" she said.

"Want to come over and paint with me this morning?" I said.

"Sure, give me half an hour."

When she arrived, we smoked a joint and organized our painting materials.

"What should we paint?" she said.

"I'm going to do a waterscape, maybe a sailboat and a fisherman," I said.

"That sounds nice. I'm going to do something abstract. By the way, have you talked to Heather yet?" she said.

"Yes, she was cool about the whole thing. I think she really likes me. We're going to get together later today, and I'm not going to touch her."

"Good idea."

I put on some jazz, and we began to paint. We were both doing small canvases. It wasn't long before we were done. We compared paintings and agreed we had both done well.

"Do you want to pick this one up tomorrow after it dries?" I said.

Just then, the phone rang. It was Heather.

"Hi, sleepyhead," I said.

"Hi. It feels so good to sleep in late."

"I've already done a painting this morning."

"Wow! I'm impressed."

We made a date to get together for dinner. I felt guilty while I was on the phone for seeking out Linda earlier.

"You'd better stick with Heather," Lisa said.

"Why?" I said.

"Because she already knows about your mental illness, and she seems to really care about you. Why is it that a guy is never satisfied with a woman once he has her? The grass is always greener on the other side."

"Same thing goes for you, sweetheart. Why couldn't you just marry me and be satisfied?" I returned jokingly.

"Let's not talk about that again. I told you, I'm not in love with you!" she said.

That shut me up. I began to roll a joint so I could forget about what Lisa had just said.

I really was in love with Lisa and would have been perfectly satisfied marrying her. I thought if I simply kept waiting, she would come around, but it wasn't happening fast enough.

"Listen, I'm going to go out for a while. I've got to get

groceries. I'll talk to you later, okay?" I said.

"Sure. I'm sorry if I hurt your feelings. I'll call you later. Have fun with Heather tonight," she said.

I was actually much more hurt than I first thought. I had known Lisa for a long time and didn't fully realize how much I was in love with her. As I walked along the grocery aisles picking out food, I displaced my hurt by thinking about Heather. Linda also came into my mind; I imagined caressing her soft blonde hair and sucking on her plump breasts. I thought to myself that I couldn't touch Heather that night. It would be hard to resist her, knowing what a good lover she was.

When I got home, I took a nap and talked to both Mikes on the phone afterward. Big Mike thought I should fuck Heather again and solidify the relationship, while Little Mike thought I should play it cool. At five o'clock, Heather showed up. She looked great; her chestnut hair flowed over her shoulders, and she was wearing a tight pair of slacks, showing off her ass.

"How has your day been so far?" I said.

"Great!" I stayed in bed and read the paper. Then I went to the club and worked out. What about your day?" she asked.

"I always feel good after doing a painting. Come to the back porch and see the new work."

She really liked my new paintings and kissed me after viewing them. I wanted to grab her right there, but I resisted the temptation and led her back out into the living room. My bag of pot was sitting right on the coffee table, but I wanted to be fairly straight for this dinner.

"You can do a hit if you want," she said as she noticed me looking at the bag.

"No, that's all right. I figured you didn't want to smoke this time," I said.

"Maybe after dinner," she said.

We went into the kitchen and talked while I cooked.

"How are you sleeping at night?" she asked.

"Pretty well; you know the medication really works, and along with the pot, I get pretty tired by evening," I said. "Does it bother you that I smoke so much pot?"

"A little, yes. But I understand self-medication. You'd be better off without it."

"I know, and I plan on quitting, but I'm addicted, and I haven't been able to quit so far."

"If you really want to, you will," she said, "but that doesn't change the way I feel about you. I really like you."

"I like you, too."

We sat down to eat and had a glass of wine with dinner. We listened to jazz as we ate, and the atmosphere was perfect. We weren't nervous around each other anymore; having made love already had broken the ice. We talked like old friends. I wanted to fuck her again and kept thinking about it as I looked into her eyes. Her eyes sparkled with excitement as she talked, and I loved the way she brushed back her hair.

"I can't wait until spring comes," she said. "I've had it with the snow."

"Me too. I would like to paint outside this summer; that should be interesting."

"I want you to sketch me again," she said. "This time in the nude."

"Sure, but I don't know how good I'll be at it."

I thought I could try to sketch her that evening, which would lead nicely into a night of romance.

"Do you want me to sketch you tonight?" I asked.

"I'd love it."

After dinner, we sat on the couch, and I smoked a little pot.

"I want some too," she said.

"Are you sure?" I said.

"Yes. Come on, give me a hit." She took a hit, and a wide smile grew on her face. I took out my sketchbook and had her sit on the other couch.

"Take your clothes off," I said.

She got up and did a striptease for me, revealing her beautiful pussy very close to my face.

"You are gorgeous," I said. "Lie on the couch now and stay very still."

She positioned herself on her side with one knee in the air, and the other leg straight out, so that her pussy was slightly exposed. I could hardly concentrate. I wanted to jump over the coffee table and fuck her right there. I began making a general outline of her body, first her legs, then her upper torso. Once I had the body well sketched, I moved to her face, which took me a long time.

"How is it coming along?" she asked.

"I'm almost done."

I wasn't particularly happy with it when I had finished, but she insisted on seeing it.

"It's good," she said.

"Not really."

"Do you want to do another one?" she asked.

"No. I want to make love to you."

"Sounds good to me."

We went into the bedroom holding hands, and she stretched out on the bed. I took my clothes off slowly, leaving my boxer shorts on. I was hard as a rock. I had her roll on her stomach and gave her a back rub, concentrating on her beautiful ass. Then I put my cock in the crack of her ass and rubbed it back and forth slowly. She turned around and put my cock in her mouth, holding my balls lightly. I fucked her mouth and shot a load right in the back of the throat.

Then we relaxed for a little while, my hand on her ass, her hand on my cock. We spoke in gentle tones, talking about how much we liked each other and how comfortable we were together. Twenty minutes later, I was able to get hard again. I told her to kneel on all fours, and I fucked her from behind, making her come twice.

"You're a good fuck," she said.

"So are you," I replied.

Exhausted, we got in the shower and washed each other lovingly. I felt like I was in love. Linda passed through my mind for a second, but I pushed the thought away. We got dressed and went into the living room. I wanted to smoke more pot but resisted again.

"I really like your friends," she said.

"What brought that up?" I asked.

"I don't know. The other night was a lot of fun. You don't see too many people with such close friends."

"All my friends have one thing in common, which overrides everything else. They all have a great sense of humor."

"I noticed that, and I want to be part of the team," she said.

"You are already. One of my ideas in graduate school was that one without laughter is oppressed, but one with laughter may not be the oppressor. It's a combination of Derrida and Marx."

"I can see that."

"It's a binary that is out of joint or off its hinges," I said.

"You and your philosophy. That shit is way over my head,"

she said.

"I try to simplify my ideas so that everyone can understand them."

"I like your poetry. It flows so nicely, and the images are beautiful."

"Flattery will get you everywhere."

We talked for another hour, until she had to go home. I gave her a long kiss goodnight and told her I would call her the next day. After she left, I took several bong hits and went to sleep. It had been a perfect day, and I slept well.

Chapter Ten

A few days later, we had a warm spell. The temperature went up to sixty degrees, and it was raining when I woke up. As I walked to the coffee shop with my slicker and umbrella, I thought about running into Linda again. During that week, I had seen her a few times, and I thought I liked her more than Heather. Linda was definitely more beautiful, but Heather was soft and lovable. I wanted to get Linda into bed to see if she would soften up and become a different person.

Linda was ambitious. She wanted to go places and be an important person. Heather was more satisfied doing what she was doing and didn't care if she rose any higher. I liked Linda's ambition. I wanted to follow her progress and watch her move up the ladder. The wind picked up as I was walking, and the rain pelted me in the face. My umbrella turned inside out at one point, and my hood blew off my head. I didn't like taking the car. This would be my exercise for the day.

Linda was already sitting in the café when I arrived. Her hair was pulled back, and she was wearing makeup, which was unusual for her.

"Hey girl, what's going on?" I said.

"You're right on time," she said.

"I didn't know I was keeping a schedule."

"You're always here about the same time every morning."

"It's a good way of having a date without really having a date."

"What's new?" she said.

"Let me get a coffee. I'll be right back," I said.

I looked around to see who else had shown up that morning, but only a few of the regulars were there. I got a large latte; I wanted a jolt from the caffeine. That morning I hadn't done my writing. I was planning on doing it as soon as I got home. I still had that nervous, excited feeling around Linda. She was so beautiful, and I always felt infatuated.

"What's on your agenda for the day?" she asked.

"I've got some writing to do, and hopefully, I'll paint a little."

"I have the afternoon off, if you want to get together?" she said.

"That would be great. Why don't you come over about four o'clock?" I suggested.

"Do you think you could paint me?" she asked.

"I'll sketch you. I haven't learned how to do portraits yet," I said.

We talked for another half hour until she had to go to class. I was very excited about her coming over. I imagined sketching her in the nude, as I had with Heather, and then fucking her. Of course, I knew it wouldn't go that way; I would probably just sketch her face and have dinner with her, but I felt we were getting closer. When I left the café, it had stopped raining, but the wind was still pretty strong.

When I returned home, I got my writing done quickly. It never took me very long. I called Little Mike, who was still asleep but got up to talk to me.

"Guess who's coming over later?" I said.

"Heather."

"No. Linda."

"You're going to get yourself in trouble."

"It's the kind of trouble I like."

"What if they find out about each other?" he asked.

"They won't. I'll make sure of that. Hey, you want to come over for a while? I've got some pot," I said.

"Sure. Give me an hour," he said. "Okay. See you."

Little Mike had the best sense of humor of all my friends. His timing was great, and he had a wonderful sense of irony. On many occasions, he was caustic and sarcastic, but he was always funny. He got to my house an hour later, like he said, with his guitar. We got the bong out, and I put some orange juice in it. I got out my keyboard, and we jammed for a while.

"Did I tell you I fucked Heather again?" I said.

"No. She must really like you. Now you're tired of her, which is why you're going after Linda. Why don't you just stick with one? We all liked Heather. She's perfect for you."

"No, she's not. I think I like Linda better. She's sharper and funnier; she keeps me on my toes. Heather is too easy. She likes me too much."

"You're impossible. How can a woman like you too much?" he said.

"I don't know. She's too easy to please. I like some resistance. Heather doesn't take control. I like a woman who dominates and is assertive."

"In other words, you want to be a slave to your woman. Where's your manhood?" he asked.

"I get bored if the woman is easily controlled. You know how it is. You're the same way."

"I'm not like that," he said.

"Yes, you are. That's why you don't stick with your women."

We smoked a little more pot and put on some jazz.

"You're really not ready to settle down yet," he said. "You'll get tired of Linda too. I'll bet anything."

"I don't know. She's different."

"They're all different at first. Then, when it becomes routine, you get bored."

He couldn't stick around too long, so he left, saying he would call me later. All I could think about was fucking Linda. I took a short nap after lunch and got ready to paint. I wanted to do a big painting of something really unique, but I couldn't think of what to do. Finally, I decided to paint a man in a triangular jail cell, all in blue. It took me two hours and turned out pretty good. I was curious as to how Linda would react to it.

She arrived right on time and looked great. Her hair was down, and she had on a dark green sweater and tight jeans.

"Hi, handsome."

"Hi yourself, beautiful."

It's still pretty warm outside, but it's raining."

"You want me to build a fire?" I asked.

"That would be great. I love your place. Look at all the paintings!" she exclaimed.

"This is the one I did today. What do you think?" I said.

"I like it, Paul. All your work is symbolic in a way."

"Yeah, I like to make people think a little bit."

We sat on the couch that partially faced the fire, and I offered her a drink. I had some red wine, which she preferred. We were sitting pretty far away from each other, but I didn't mind. I figured something might happen later.

"Is that your sketchbook?" she asked.

"Yes, but the work is not very professional."

"Let me see."

"All right."

"Who's this?" she said as she arrived at Heather's pictures.

"Oh, just a model I used. Actually, she's a friend of mine."

"She must be a pretty good friend."

"Not really," I said.

I took the book out of her hands and closed it, setting it on the coffee table.

"How do you like the wine?" I said.

"It's delicious. You have very good taste," she said.

"Would you like to pose for me?" I asked.

"Sure, but with my clothes on," she laughed.

"Of course."

I led her over to the other couch and put her in a stretched-out position, with her head resting on her hand. For about twenty minutes, I sketched her and then told her she could relax.

"It's not very good," I declared.

"Let me see."

"No, I'd rather you didn't."

"Oh, come on. I don't care. This is the first time anybody has ever drawn me."

"All right," I said, passing her the book.

"It's fine," she said.

"Next time will be better," I said.

"Can I keep it?" she said.

"Sure."

We sat close together this time and talked about various things. I decided I would try to kiss her. As she was talking, I put my hand under her chin, turned her face toward mine, and kissed her. She closed her eyes and opened her mouth, letting me slip my tongue inside. After kissing for a minute, we pulled apart.

"You're a good kisser," she said.

"So are you," I said. "Do you want to continue?"

"Yes."

We kissed some more, and I put my hand on her breast, which she let me keep there. I thought she might let me go all the way at this point. I massaged both her breasts and slipped my hand under her sweater and blouse. She wasn't wearing a bra. She had medium-sized breasts, plump and delicious. I pulled up her blouse and began sucking on her tits. Then I put my hand between her legs, but she pushed it away.

"Easy boy," she whispered in my ear.

I decided to slow down, so I pulled her sweater down and began to kiss her again.

"I love you," I said, but why I said it, I don't know.

"It's too early for that," she said.

I pulled away from her and sat upright, brushing my hair with my hand.

"Let's just talk for a while," I said.

"Sure."

"How long has it been since you've been in a relationship," I asked.

"A while."

"Were you hurt?" I replied.

"Yes."

"I won't hurt you."

"That's what they all say."

"Do you want something to eat?" I said.

"Yes, please."

"I've got some frozen steaks."

"Great, but can I cook them?" she asked.

"Sure, if you want to."

We went into the kitchen. The change of scenery was what we needed. I took out the steaks and put them in the microwave.

I made some instant mashed potatoes while she cooked the steaks. It didn't take long to prepare our meal.

The two of us sat in front of the television and watched the news. She told me she liked to keep up with current events. I kissed her again after dinner, but we had lost the moment. There wouldn't be any more fooling around that evening.

"I have to go," she said.

"Okay. I'll probably see you at the café in the morning. After she left, I smoked some pot and called Lisa, who wasn't home. I thought our date had gone pretty well, and I went to bed fantasizing about Linda.

Chapter Eleven

The next day the cold air returned with a vengeance, and so did the snow. I made coffee first thing in the morning and had a cigarette while I waited for it to brew. I turned on the news and caught up again with the events from the day before. The house was filled with the smell of fresh coffee and smoke, but my nose didn't work very well anyway. I poured myself a cup of coffee and sat down to write. I was writing a novel about an alcoholic who had lost everything except his teaching job and was ready to commit suicide. I wrote for about half an hour and decided that was enough. I was looking forward to meeting Linda, so I showered quickly and got dressed.

When I walked outside, the snow whipped against my face and I decided to drive to the café for the first time in a long time. I was a bit earlier than usual, and Linda wasn't there yet. Mark was there so I sat with him.

"Hey, what's going on?" he said.

"Man, it's nasty out there."

"Typical Syracuse weather."

"What are you working on?" I said.

"Everything is based on religion," he said.

"I disagree, but I'm not going to get into an argument. I'm waiting for Linda."

I got myself a latte and sat back down. The café didn't have many people in it.

"Did you guys get together last night?" Mark said.

"We sure did. It was great. I sketched her. Then we had dinner."

"In the nude?" he asked.

"No, but we did kiss for a while."

"It won't be long then," he said.

Linda walked in half an hour later with a big smile on her face. Her face was red from the cold, and her hair was pulled back again.

"Hi, you guys."

"What's up, girl?" I said.

"This weather is miserable," she said.

"I've got to go," Mark said. "I'll see you two later."

Linda got a cup of coffee and sat down, her smile still on her face.

"I had a great time last night," she said.

"So did I. Do you want to get together again this weekend?" I asked.

"Sure."

I thought about Heather for a split second. She would want to come over during the weekend as well. I was horny as usual that morning and figured I could fuck Heather that night.

"I want you to sketch my whole body next time," Linda said.

"In the nude?" I said.

"Semi-nude, just wearing my bra and panties."

"Are you sure?" I said.

"Yes. It's no big deal. Is it?' she said.

"No, of course not."

"I want you to make me part of your collection."

I was excited to hear her talk that way. I was making inroads, and that felt good. Now I had some problems. It seemed that both women wanted to get serious with me, and sooner or later, I would have to make a decision. Linda had to go to class, and I left the café shortly after she did.

When I got home, there was a message from Lisa on my recorder. She wanted to come over and paint. I called her and invited her over. I wanted to talk to her about my situation with the women. She showed up half an hour later, wearing her tight jeans, and I could see the outline of her pussy in her crotch. I cleaned out the bong, and we did a few hits while we talked.

"I think Linda wants to fuck me," I said.

"How do you know?" she queried.

"She came over last night, and while we were making out, she said, 'Not yet.'"

"Do you like her better than Heather?" said Lisa.

"I think so, but I like Heather too. I don't know what to do."

"I know what you're going to do."

"What's that?" she asked.

"You're going to fuck them both for a while until it blows up in your face."

"I thought about that. Mike says the same thing."

I looked out the window at the snow clinging to the trees and imagined fucking Linda. The conquest was everything. Linda was much more of a challenge than Heather and probably more difficult to keep, which intrigued me.

"Maybe I should drop Heather and go out with Linda."

"I can't tell you what to do. You have to decide for yourself."

"I think I'm going to try to get Linda into bed before I decide anything."

"I want to meet this Linda. She sounds too good to be true."

"Do you feel like painting?" I asked.

"Sure."

We got organized and painted for about an hour. I was trying something new, which involved striations of colors with no particular design. The outcome was a feeling of water or sky. Every day I was gaining more control with the paintbrush; as I experimented, I taught myself new things.

"Let's have something to eat. Then I have to go," she said.

We had a sandwich. Then she left. The morning had been productive, but now, I was left alone with my fantasies. I took a nap and woke up feeling reenergized. I smoked some pot, as I usually did upon awakening, and called Little Mike.

"Hey, what's up?" he said.

"My dick."

"Did you fuck Heather again last night?" he replied.

"No. Linda came over."

"Did you fuck her?" he said.

"No. We just made out."

"It won't be long now."

"We'll see. I'm not as confident with Linda as I am with Heather."

"Can I come over for a while?" he asked.

"Sure. That's why I was calling."

Half an hour later, Mike showed up. He hadn't bothered to shave as he wasn't working that evening. He looked like a true rebel. I cleaned out the bong and put some orange juice in it.

"This pot is amazing," he said. "You only need one or two hits."

"It's homegrown from up north."

"Where's your guitar?" he said.

"I'll get it," I said.

He played the guitar for a while, showing me some new riffs he had been working on. He was really getting good. He knew how to make that guitar sing. I got out my keyboard and we jammed for a while. I played the background for him as he went off into the wilderness. After we played, we smoked a little more and Mike played DJ.

"Hey, what's going on with you and Alicia?" I said.

"Who knows; we just fuck each other and go on our merry way."

"You two used to really like each other."

"We still do, I guess, but not as much as we used to. I'm looking elsewhere. The great thing about Alicia is that she doesn't demand anything from me," he said.

"That probably means she's looking elsewhere too."

"Oh, I'm sure. That's all right."

Mike was cool. He didn't worry about women too much. He could go for long periods of time without a girlfriend. He was a bit of a playboy like me, but a few years younger. I was getting to the age of wanting to settle down. He left an hour or so later, high as hell, and feeling good. I wanted to call Heather, but I didn't want to do it high. I decided to call her the next morning instead, and I went to bed early that night.

I got up very early the next day and put on a pot of coffee as usual. I smoked a cigarette and, when the coffee was ready, sat down to write. After I wrote, I called Heather, who was still sleeping.

"I'm sorry to wake you, sweetheart. I'll call you later."

"No. That's all right. It's about time for me to get up anyway."

"I was thinking about you last night," I said.

"I thought about you too."

"How did you sleep?" I asked.

"Pretty well, but I woke up in the middle of the night for a couple of hours."

"I hate that," I said. "I find that if I masturbate, I go right back to sleep."

"I needed you to be here with me," she said.

"That can be arranged."

We talked for a little while longer, and I invited her over for dinner. She accepted graciously, and for the rest of the day all I could think about was getting laid.

I didn't know if I should get high or not before going to the coffee shop, knowing Linda would be there. I decided to go straight. She still didn't know how much I smoked. I shaved and showered, and dressed with about five layers of clothes. The wind was calm when I walked outside, but it was very cold. The snow crunched under my feet. Most of the sidewalks were not shoveled.

Mark was at the café when I arrived. He was so involved in his reading, he didn't even see me come in.

"Hey, Mr. Philosopher, what's up?" I said.

"Just hanging out," he said.

"When was the last time you got laid?" I said.

"It's been a while."

"All work and no play..."

"I'm thinking about somebody."

"Good! Now all you have to do is ask her out."

"I will in good time."

"Don't hesitate too long. She'll lose interest."

Just then, Linda walked in. Her hair was down, and she was dressed in her dark green coat again. She looked as fresh as a daisy.

"Hey guys," she said.

"What's up, girl?" I said.

She went to get a cappuccino and wiggled her ass as she walked. She knew she could drive men crazy. When she came back, she had a big smile on her face.

"I framed that sketch of yours," she said.

"Well, why don't you wait until I do a better one?" I said.

"Too late. Besides, I like the one you did."

"I have to go to teach. I'll see you two tomorrow," Mark said.

"All right, but remember what I said."

"What did you tell him?" she said.

"Oh, he's interested in this girl, but he's afraid to ask her out, so I told him not to hesitate."

"He's a good-looking man. He shouldn't have any trouble," Linda said.

"He needs to be more confident. He has always got his face buried in a book. He's got a sense of humor, but he doesn't know how to talk to women."

"And you do?" she smiled.

"Yes, I do," I laughed.

"Tell me about your last girlfriend."

I hesitated.

"Well, her name is Laura, and she is very beautiful. I idealized her. I was too infatuated to really see her as she was. She is a few years older than I am and has her shit together. I couldn't see straight for a long time, I was so in love.

"What happened?" she probed.

"There was another man, and she picked him."

"You must have been devastated."

"I was for a while, but then as I put things in perspective, I decided I was better off without her."

"Why?" she asked.

"She said she was always depressed. She spent a fortune on

therapy, something I overlooked when we were dating."

I looked into Linda's eyes, and they were sparkling. She was so full of life. I was crazy about her too, but not as I had been with Laura. I had learned a thing or two.

"She was a little neurotic," I said.

"You can fall in love with someone who's neurotic."

"Yes, but can you live with them in the long term?" I said.

"You're right. I guess it must be very difficult. It would probably be like living with an alcoholic," she said.

My heart took a beat when she said that. I wondered how she would feel if she knew how much pot I smoked. I felt like telling her that I smoked, but I figured it would be better if I held off for a while.

"What about your last boyfriend?" I said.

"You're not going to believe this, but he was a high school dropout."

"What was so interesting about him?" I returned.

"He was cool. He didn't give a damn about what anybody else thought."

"What's so cool about that?" I said.

"I don't know. He's very independent. He doesn't follow society's norms."

"That does surprise me. I wouldn't have figured you to like bad boys."

"There's a wicked side to me," she smiled.

"Why did you break up?" I said.

"We grew in different ways. I wanted something else out of life."

"Such as?" I continued.

"An education for one thing."

"You grew up and he didn't."

"I wouldn't put it that way. We grew in different directions."

"How did he grow?" I said.

"He wanted to go to the west coast and open his own business. He had some money."

"Did he do that?" I questioned.

"Not yet."

"Dreams are one thing. Actions are another," I said.

I could tell she was beginning to get irritated by my questions; I think she felt she was being interrogated, so I let it go. She kept her cool though. We were still feeling each other out, and she knew that.

"I have to go to class. Do you want to get together later?" she said.

"I can't tonight. Maybe tomorrow. I'd like to sketch you again."

"I'd like that."

We parted, and I went home to paint. The wind had picked up and fine snow was falling. I couldn't wait to get home. The bong was dirty from the night before, so I cleaned it out, taking it apart and giving it a good scrubbing. I put ice in it with a little water and took a few hits off of it. That was all I needed.

I set up a canvas and organized my paints. Half an hour later, I was done with a small painting. As soon as I was done, I called Lisa.

"What does it look like?" she asked.

"I mixed a lot of turpentine with the oils and let it bleed across the canvas. It looks like a pond with some sort of crazy duck on it."

"Cool."

"Yeah, it turned out great. What are you doing? Can you

come over for a while?" I said.

"For an hour or so," she said.

"See you soon."

She showed up an hour later, wearing her tight jeans and a sweatshirt. Her eyes were sparkling, and she was in a good mood.

"Let me see it," she said.

I took her to the back porch where I was doing my paintings and showed her the new canvas.

"It's great," she said.

"Thanks. I like it too."

"Have you got any pot?" she asked.

"When don't I have some?"

We sat on the back porch and looked at the snow falling as we smoked.

"How's your little boyfriend?" I said.

"He's exasperating," she said.

"Why?"

"He doesn't want to do anything with his life. He's always depressed."

"Why don't you break up with him? That might motivate him."

"I already threatened I would."

Lisa had a funny habit of doing stretching exercises when she got high. She got on the floor and pulled her knees over her head, her ass sticking up in the air. Her panties were exposed a bit, and I wanted to fuck her right there. Then she did a split and bent over forwards, pressing her tits against the floor.

"I want to fuck you," I said.

"It would ruin our friendship," she said.

"No, it wouldn't."

"Yes, it would."

"I can't get anywhere with you!" I exasperated.

"Can't you just accept our relationship the way it is?" she said.

"No."

"Well, you're going to have to."

"What if I told you that you can't come over any more," I said.

"You wouldn't do that."

"You're right. I wouldn't."

She sat back down on the couch, realizing she was making me horny. She liked to tease me. She got off on it.

"Heather is coming over tonight," I said.

"Well, you can fuck her. What are you worried about?" she said.

"I want to fuck you."

"You want to fuck everybody."

"Is there anything wrong with that?" I asked.

"Yes."

"I love you, Lisa. You know that. There's nothing wrong with wanting to fuck someone you love."

We smoked some more pot and were silent for a while. Through the frosted windows, I watched the snow falling and thought about Heather and Linda. These were bountiful days, and I thought that soon I would probably be down to zero girlfriends. That's why I held on to Lisa, because no matter what, I considered her my girlfriend, and she made me feel complete. My friends thought that because I wasn't fucking her that she wasn't really my girlfriend, but I didn't feel that way. Also, there was always the hope that she would come around one day.

"Are you cooking for Heather tonight?" she said.

"Probably."

"You don't sound very enthusiastic."

"I'm not."

"I thought you were looking forward to getting laid."

"I'm more interested in Linda."

"That's only because you haven't fucked her yet."

"No. I really find her more interesting and more exciting."

"But you haven't told her anything about yourself."

"True, and I'm not going to for a while either."

"Not until you've fucked her."

"Something like that."

Lisa gave me a disdainful look as if she were disappointed in me.

"I have to go," she said.

"I'll call you later," I said.

Chapter Twelve

In the afternoon, I did some grocery shopping, selecting a few specialty foods to impress Heather. The snow had stopped falling, but the wind had freshened. I watered the plants when I got home and set the mood with my lamps. I vacuumed the rug and dusted the house, giving the place a new look. I knew Heather didn't care if I was high, so I took a few hits off the bong. I was horny as hell, so I watched a porno movie for a few minutes and got a hard-on.

Heather showed up at about four o'clock. She was wearing tan dress pants and a matching blouse, and for the first time, she was wearing makeup. She looked radiant. I took off her coat and offered her a glass of wine.

"I want to see what you've done since I was last here," she said.

"It's on the back porch."

I took her to the back porch and we sat on the couch.

"Beautiful," she said.

"Thanks. I like it too."

I kissed her before she could say another word, and in a minute, we were completely naked. I licked her pussy until she came. Then I fucked the shit out of her. She came three times.

"I need a break," she said.

"You like that, don't you?" I teased.

"What?" she said.

"When I fuck you really hard."

"Yeah, you've got a lot of energy."

"It comes naturally. I come from a long line of Italian lovers."

"So that's it."

"What did you think it was?" I said.

"I thought maybe it was the Wheaties?" she joked.

"No. I'm strictly a Raisin Bran man."

"And a poet."

"That too."

"Let's take a shower," she said.

"Okay."

We took a nice, long hot shower, and I had her lean against the wall while I inserted my cock from behind. She had a nice tight ass. I loved to watch it while I fucked her from behind. I made her come again, and she screamed out in ecstasy. Then she got on her knees and sucked me off. I came in her mouth, which is my favorite thing to do.

"That was great," I said.

"Yeah, I could do this every day," she said.

I took that as a hint that she wanted to get more serious. That scared me a little bit, but I decided to play along.

"We can do this every day," I said.

"Are you sure?" she said.

"I really like you, Heather. Maybe it's time to get more involved."

"We're starting pretty fast, but it feels right to me," she said.

"Me too."

It occurred to me, of course, that if I saw Heather every day, it would be impossible to see Linda. I didn't want to think about it at that moment, so I put it out of my mind. We got dressed, and I went into the kitchen to cook while Heather played with the stereo. She took a few hits of pot and was laughing the rest of the evening. We made love one more time after dinner and experimented with several new positions. Heather left at about nine o'clock, and I fell into bed exhausted.

The next morning, I got up early and wrote a poem about being caught between two women. I noticed after writing it that I was leaning more toward Linda than Heather. I took a nice hot shower and got ready to go to the coffee shop. I loved my routine; I didn't have to rush off to work, and I could paint to my heart's content. Linda was already there when I arrived. She had her hair in a bun and was wearing her reading glasses. I wanted to tear off those glasses and pull her hair down like in the movies with the wild librarians.

"Hey, what's up?" I said.
"Hi," she said in a sweet tone.
"Looks like you're hard at work."
"Yeah, I've got a paper due in a week."
"Well, at least you're not waiting till the last minute. Let me get a coffee. I'll be right back."

I sat down and looked at her beautiful face. She seemed serene and focused; I loved an intellectual woman.
"I saw Mark earlier," she said.
"Was he studying?" I asked.
"Of course."
"That boy better get his head out of the books. There's so much more in the world."
"He's not like you."
"He needs a woman."
"Some men never have a woman," she said.
"He will," I said. "I think she'll be a bookworm like him."

"What about you? What kind of a woman will you end up with?" she replied.

"I don't know, someone like you maybe."

"How flattering."

"No. I'm serious. She's got to be smart, well educated, but cool at the same time."

"I didn't know I was cool."

"You are, definitely."

"What is cool anyway?" she said.

"I don't know. It's an instinctive knowledge of human nature and an ability to handle most situations without losing one's cool."

She laughed. I loved to hear her laugh. The sound she made was like a mating call. It accentuated her beauty, and I just wanted to grab her. She was cool too. She knew she was beautiful and used it to her advantage. She was unobtainable. Even if one married her, she could not be owned, and that was attractive. I was beginning to fall in love with her. I wanted to be with her all the time, to possess what I could not possess.

"Do you want to come over this evening?" I said.

"I can't. I really have to work on this paper."

"I could help you with it."

"I appreciate that, but I should do it by myself."

"Of course."

Half an hour later, we parted. On the way home, the wind chilled me to the bone, and all I could think about was Linda. She was truly remarkable, and I feared I could not have her. When I got home, I rolled a joint and prepared a canvas. I was in a green period, which I didn't even realize until I looked over my latest paintings.

I sketched my face on the canvas and painted it green; to my great surprise, it resembled me considerably. I called Lisa to see what she was up to and invited her over. She hadn't showered yet and said it would take her an hour to arrive. I made some coffee and put Miles Davis on the stereo. I thought about Linda and Heather and decided I was in love with Linda. I had to tell Heather that I was no longer interested.

Heather wanted to come over that night though, and I wanted to get laid. I also thought that perhaps I had better wait to break up with Heather until I had fucked Linda. Mike's words haunted me; he had said I would end up losing them both, and now that seemed quite possible.

Lisa showed up a little later, and she looked great as usual. I gave her a kiss on the cheek and grabbed her ass.

"Come on. Let's go to the back porch. I want to show you my first self-portrait."

"You actually did a self-portrait? How did it turn out?" she asked.

"Come on. I'll show you."

"Wow! It really looks like you. But why is it totally green?" she asked.

"I don't know really. I think I'm going through a green period."

"I like it," she said.

"It's only my first one; I'll get better at it."

We smoked some pot, and she got on the floor to do some exercises.

"I love it when you stick your ass in the air," I said.

"No comments."

"Okay."

"What's the latest on your love triangle?" she said.

"I think I'm going to break up with Heather and just go out with Linda."

"Are you going to fuck Linda before you break up with Heather?" she said.

"I don't think so."

"You're feeling guilty, aren't you?" she asked.

"What do you mean?"

"By leading on Heather."

"I guess so."

"You'll be doing the right thing."

"But what if Linda doesn't want to fuck me?" I replied.

"You can always go back to Heather."

"I doubt it."

Lisa spread her legs and bent forwards, pressing her firm tits against the floor. While she wasn't looking, I rubbed my cock a little bit. Her ass was perfect. I could see the outline of her panties through her tight jeans.

"I think Heather wants to get serious with me. I could use a steady girlfriend," I said.

"Now you're changing your mind again," she said.

"I can't help it. It's confusing."

"Why don't you keep going the way you're going and see how things play out?" she suggested.

"Maybe you're right. But how can I see Linda if Heather's over here all the time?" I said.

"Don't have her over that much."

"Yeah, I guess you're right."

Lisa stayed around for another hour or so, then left, high as a kite. I took a short nap and made myself a sandwich. I wanted to call Heather at work and set something up for that evening, but then I changed my mind. I was frustrated as usual and spent the rest of the afternoon and evening watching movies on cable.

Chapter Twelve

I waited a few days before returning to the coffee shop and didn't call Heather either. I needed time to think. March came in like a lion. The snow kept coming, and it was bitterly cold. This was the time of year when everyone got sick of the weather and complained all the time. The painting was going well. I kept experimenting and developing new techniques. I missed Linda terribly; it was time to go see her again. One Friday, I returned to the coffee shop, but Linda wasn't there. I sat by myself and did a bit of writing. An hour later, Linda walked in.

"Hi, stranger," she said.

"Hi yourself."

"What have you been up to?" she asked.

"I've been doing a lot of painting."

"I missed you," she said.

"I missed you too," I said.

We sat for an hour and talked. Our conversation was not that intimate; we were feeling each other out. When we parted, I kissed her on the cheek and told her I would meet her the next day. My feelings for her were stronger than ever, and I thought that morning I would let Heather go. I was taking my time with Linda. I wanted to present myself as a challenge.

The opportunity of having a good relationship excited me. I thought that perhaps I could marry her.

She was playing it cool too. Her instincts were good. If she had come on too strong, I would have run. When I got home, I called Heather at work.

"Hi, sweetheart," I said.

"What are you doing?" she asked.

"I'm getting ready to paint, but I'd like to see you tonight."

"Sure. What time?" she said.

"How about five?" I replied.

"Perfect."

Heather was such a good fuck, I couldn't stay away from her. She moaned, and groaned, and screamed when she had an orgasm. For the rest of the day, all I could think about was fucking Heather. Lisa came over for half an hour to get high and just shook her head when I told her my plans.

Heather showed up right on time. She was wearing tight jeans and a blue sweater to match. Her hair was down as usual, and it was curly. She looked so damn sexy.

Hi, beautiful," I said.

"Hi, handsome."

"How did your day go?" I asked.

"One patient gave me a hard time today. He kept following me around."

"I must have given you a hard time too."

"No, you were sane. It was a pleasure to have you around."

"Do you want to see my new painting?" I asked.

"I'd love to."

I took her to the back porch and showed it to her.

"Wow!" was all she said.

"Sit down, relax. I'm going to smoke a little."

"I'll take a hit too," she said.

We got stoned and started kissing. I was hard as a rock.

"Let's go into the bedroom," she said.

I gave her a backrub, sitting on her ass, my cock positioned between her cheeks. She flipped over, and I rubbed her stomach and chest, my balls aching. I licked her pussy, rubbing her g-spot with my middle finger. When she came, she arched her back and screamed out. I couldn't wait any longer. I put my cock in her and pumped as slowly as I could, saving myself. Her eyes were closed, and she was twisting her nipples. I wanted to come in her mouth, and I told her so.

"Make me come again," she said.

I thrust harder and harder, gritting my teeth as if I were trying to hurt her. I came in her mouth, and she gagged on my come.

"I came at the same time you did. That's never happened to me before," she said.

"It doesn't happen very often," I said, lying back exhausted.

"Let's fuck again," she said.

"What? Are you kidding? I can barely move."

"I'll let you rest for a while."

I rolled over and closed my eyes. In a minute, I was sleeping. When I awakened, half an hour later, I found Heather in the living room watching TV.

"Hi," I said.

"Hi, studly."

"Sorry, I was pooped out."

"You were great."

"Thanks for always boosting my ego. You must be the nicest woman I've ever gone out with."

"I doubt it, but it's a very sweet thought."

We relaxed in the living room for a while. Then I made dinner. Our conversation was rarely intellectual, though she knew quite a lot about psychological theory. Instead, we talked about personal matters: how each of us felt about certain things.

"Do you want to have children?" she asked.

"I think so. What about you?" I asked.

"Definitely. Three at least."

"That's a good number. There are three boys in my family."

"We have two girls and two boys. The last boy wasn't really planned."

"Which one are you?" I asked.

"I'm the oldest."

"No wonder you're so mature and responsible."

"What about you?" she asked.

"I have a twin and an older brother."

"You're a twin?" she said.

"Fraternal. And I'm better looking, though he'll tell you the opposite."

"Are you a lot alike?" she pressed.

"We're very different," I said.

"Are you close?" she said.

"Yes."

"Are you close to your brothers and sisters?" I asked while we were still in bed.

"I'm closest to my sister."

"Did you have to babysit a lot when you were growing up?" I asked.

"Yeah, but I didn't mind. It came to me naturally," she said.

We talked for another hour or so before she went home. She asked me if she could spend the night, but I said not yet. I realized she was thinking about marriage. We were moving very quickly into this relationship. I knew I didn't want to marry her, though I thought she would make someone a very good wife. I thought I could marry Linda, but we hadn't got anywhere near that far.

I went to bed thinking about both of them and fell quickly into a deep sleep. The next morning, I followed my usual routine. I put on a pot of coffee, lit a cigarette, and did some writing. I didn't want to go to the coffee shop high, so I postponed my smoking.

Linda was studying when I arrived, and she didn't even see me come in.

"You really are into it today," I said.

Oh, hi Paul. Yeah, this is pretty intense."

"What is it?" I asked.

"Feminist theory."

"Some of that is good stuff, and like everything else, some of it is garbage," I said.

"This is all right," she said.

"Let me get a latte; I'll be right back," I said.

I looked around the café and said hi to a few of the regulars. It was too cold out for a large crowd. Linda looked great as usual. She had her hair pulled back and was wearing an elegant white sweater.

"You have a big smile on your face this morning," she said.

"I slept well," I said, thinking about how I had fucked Heather.

"What are you up to today?" she said.

Well, I've already done my writing. I hope to do a painting or two later."

"You never deviate from your routine."

"I like my routine; I feel very productive."

"What paintings have you done lately?"

"I did a self-portrait in green. Did I tell you about it?" I asked.

"How did it turn out?" she said.

"It's different. I like it."

"You still haven't painted me."

"Why don't you come over tonight," I suggested.
"Okay, about what time?" she said.
"How about six?" I suggested.
"Perfect."

I had a hard-on just making a date with her. I thought this might be my lucky night. We talked for about half an hour. Then I let her get back to her work. I walked outside and noticed the wind had let up considerably. It was a pleasant walk home. All I could think about was fucking Linda.

There was a message from Lisa when I arrived home. She said she wanted to paint a little. I called her and told her to come over. I was thinking that I loved Linda for her cool in our relationship. She didn't chase after me or fall in love, which made her a challenge. I was going to tell Lisa again that I favored Linda over Heather, but I knew Lisa would laugh.

When Lisa arrived, I had a pot of coffee ready. We sat on the back porch and looked out over the backyard. It was overcast, but the reflection from the snow made the porch bright.

"I saw Linda this morning," I said.
"How did that go?" she asked.
"I really like her. We get along so well."
"Are you still going to drop Heather?" she said.
"I think so."
"Why can't you make up your mind?" she pressed.
"Because I don't want to drop Heather and lose Linda at the same time."
"Love has risks," she said. "You don't love Heather. What's the point of going out with her? You know you are going to drop her eventually."
"I know, but I can't seem to do it. What about you? You're not in love either. That doesn't stop you from fucking all the

time."

I could see we were starting to get into a fight, so I loaded up the bong and took a big hit. That calmed me down, and I relaxed while Lisa took a hit. Lisa and I were like a married couple. We said what was on our minds, and we fought freely. Had she been about five years older, we probably would have been married, but she was still young and looking for something that didn't exist. Disillusionment is the biggest part of maturity, and she still harbored many illusions. I believed in love, but I was also skeptical.

"Until I fall in love, I'm going to continue to fuck Jason or whoever comes along," she said.

"So, what's different about my situation?" I asked.

"You're in love!" she exclaimed.

"But I don't know if she's in love with me."

"Well, then wait. I can't convince you of anything anyway."

"You're not right about that," I said. "Let's paint."

I took out a couple of new canvases. I was too lazy to stretch my own anymore. I wanted to paint a face again, but not my own, some strange face hardly seemed human. I began by combining four or five colors on my brush and following the general contours of a face. The effect was magnificent.

"That's interesting," she said.

She was doing some sort of bizarre landscape, which was also multicolored.

"Yours is cool too," I said.

After we painted, I wanted to take a nap, and Lisa left to get some sleep as well before going to work. I relaxed all afternoon, talking to my friends on the phone and listening to jazz.

At six o'clock, Linda showed up, looking beautiful as usual. She was wearing tight jeans and a deep blue sweater. I had smoked some pot, but I wasn't too high. I was worried that she wouldn't go out with me as soon as she found out how much pot I smoked. I had aired out the apartment and put away the paraphernalia, but I was still worried.

"Are you hungry, sweetheart?" I said.

"No. I just had a big salad."

"I have a question for you."

"Shoot."

"Do you smoke pot?" I asked.

"Once in a while."

"Would you like to smoke some now?" I said.

"Sure. Why not?" she replied.

I took her to the back porch and pulled out the bong.

"I see you're into it," she said.

"Not all the time or anything," I said.

"Are these your latest paintings?" she said.

"Yes. What do you think?" I hazarded.

"I love them."

I loaded up the bong and handed it to her. She took a big hit and started coughing.

"Easy, girl," I said.

She passed it to me and I took a hit.

"You're an expert," she said.

"I've had a little practice."

"My ex-boyfriend smoked pot."

I thought perhaps it was one of the reasons she had broken up with him, but I wasn't going to worry about it.

"Do you paint straight or sober?" she asked.

"I write sober and I paint stoned, but I'm going to quit smoking pot soon. I'm getting sick of it."

"A lot of artists work under the influence," she said.

"It's true, but I don't think it necessarily helps their work."

"Why do you paint stoned then?" she asked.

"It motivates me and inspires me; at least, that's how it began."

We went out to the living room, and I put some jazz on the stereo. She was pretty high after several hits, and I figured she would loosen up considerably. I started kissing her, thrusting my tongue deep inside her mouth. She responded with a groan. I put my hand between her legs, but she pushed it away. Suddenly, there was a knock on the door.

"I wonder who that could be?" I said.

I went to open the door, and there stood Heather, looking right at Linda.

"I was in the neighborhood, so I thought I would stop by, but I see you're busy."

"Nonsense! Come on in," I said, turning perfectly red in the face.

"No, I've really got to go. I just stopped by to say hi."

"I'll call you later," I said.

Heather left, and I was shaking like a leaf as I sat down next to Linda.

"Who was that?" she questioned.

"Just a friend."

"Are you sure about that? She seemed shocked to see me."

"Well, we dated for a while, but it's over with now."

Linda didn't say another word. She was making me feel nervous. I was trying to think up a good story, but I figured I'd better keep my mouth shut. I took a hit off the bong and offered Linda a hit, which she declined.

After a couple of minutes, I simply said, "I'll tell you about

Heather some other time, but it's over with really."

"She's pretty. Is she nice?" she asked.

"Very nice, but I'd rather not talk about her right now."

I wanted to kiss Linda, or actually fuck her, but I knew I couldn't do it after what had happened. I thought about what Little Mike had said; now it haunted me. I had probably already lost Heather, and now I was likely to lose Linda as well. Conversation was difficult at that moment, so I decided to tell Linda that I was tired and wanted to end the evening.

"I'll see you tomorrow at the coffee shop," I said.

"All right. Thanks for the nice evening," she said as she left.

My mind was racing for a while as I tried to settle down to sleep. I was angry with myself. There was no one else to blame for my stupidity. I was hoping to salvage my relationship with Linda, but figured it was definitely over with Heather. I finally got to sleep, but it was a restless night, as I kept waking up from time to time until morning.

Chapter Thirteen

I got up early, frustrated and tired, so I took a long hot shower to help relax my muscles. I kept thinking of things to say to Linda, and also Heather, though nothing I thought of sounded any good. If I insisted to Linda that my relationship with Heather was really over and let Heather go, perhaps I could keep the one I liked best. When I arrived at the coffee shop, Linda wasn't there, and I worried she wouldn't show up. I had brought my notebook with me and sat down to write. Everything I wrote that morning sounded trite, so I gave up and sipped my coffee. To my great relief, Linda showed up.

"Hi, beautiful. How are you doing this morning?" I said.

"I didn't sleep well last night, and I couldn't get out of bed this morning."

"Sorry to hear that."

"Let me get a coffee," she said. "I'll be right back."

I thought immediately that the reason she couldn't sleep was what had happened the previous evening. Then I thought that perhaps Heather's showing up might work to my advantage. Linda might be jealous, which could further her interest in me. When she came back, I noticed she did look tired.

"Why couldn't you sleep last night? I said.

"I've been stressed out over my schoolwork, and I think I drank too much coffee."

"Did you have bad dreams?" I said.

"No, I was just tossing and turning all night. How did you

sleep?" she asked.

"I slept pretty well. That pot knocks me out."

"Maybe that's why I couldn't sleep," she said. "I'm not used to it."

She seemed pretty stressed out. I knew how it felt to go without sleep. I wanted to make her feel at ease, say something that would comfort her, but I couldn't think of anything. She sipped on her coffee as though she couldn't get enough of it, and her hands were cold.

"You can nap this afternoon," I finally said.

"No, I have class this afternoon."

"Is anything else troubling you?" I urged.

"Not really. I'm pretty easygoing, you know," she said.

"I've noticed that."

She wasn't going to bring up Heather, and neither was I.

"Just leave it alone," I said to myself.

We chatted for a few more minutes. Then she left for class. I wished we had talked about Heather, so that I could have reassured Linda that it was over with her. On my way home, the wind was blowing, and it was cold. All I thought about was what I was going to say to Heather, because I still wanted to get laid.

When I got home, I smoked some pot and prepared a canvas. I called Lisa and told her what had happened. I was expecting her to say I told you so, but she didn't.

"You have to make a decision now. You can't put it off any longer," she said.

"I know, I know. I'm going to break up with Heather, if she's even talking to me anymore."

I asked Lisa if she wanted to come over to paint, but she had things to do. Then I called Little Mike, who was still sleeping, but he said he would be over in an hour. I wanted to call Heather, but kept putting if off. Mike showed up on time. He was in a good mood and wanted to smoke some pot.

"Here, let me buy an eighth off you," he said. "I can't get any from my regular supplier."

"Sure, but this stuff is expensive."

We smoked a little, and I told him what had happened the day before.

"They love the competition," he said.

"That's not what you said before."

"You watch. Heather will be all over you; just don't call her for a couple days."

I laughed to myself. None of my friends were involved in a solid, lasting relationship, yet they were full of advice. I thought I had better go with my own instincts, but I really didn't know what to do. I wanted to call Heather and explain things, but I was afraid to. Maybe I should wait a few days. On the other hand, perhaps I should let Heather go and concentrate on Linda, whom I liked better. I was really confused, and Mike wasn't making things better.

"I feel like calling Heather now," I said.

"That's your dick talking."

"No, I'm serious. I should simply explain to her that Linda is a friend who came over to look at my paintings."

"You could probably get away with that, but if you try to explain, she might think something else is going on."

"You're a pain in the ass. You know that?" I said while laughing.

We smoked some more, and Mike brought out the guitar. He was always working on something new, and he let me hear some of it. The notes floated by like clouds that changed with the wind.

There was nothing solid about them, but they were beautiful. I compared the notes to paintings, which seemed immovable but were not. The eye moves over them, and the paintings are not still either. A piece of art is never still. Like language, it is constantly in motion and, therefore, part of nature. We seek permanence, but it always eludes us.

Mike stopped playing after a while, and we had something to eat. He was funny as hell when he was high, and we laughed for several hours as we listened to jazz. After he left, I took a nap and dreamed I was having a fight with Heather.

When I awakened, I thought I had better call her. I was nervous as I dialed her number at work. She was there but said she was too busy to talk and would call me after work. She didn't sound upset.

I went out to the back porch to smoke and think about my predicament. When I got high, nothing seemed to matter. The problem would be resolved easily, and I was in total control. I decided I would break up with Heather and tried to think of the words I would use. I felt like a heel, but there was nothing else I could do. I thought maybe I would do it over the phone, but then I figured I had better do it in person. I knew Heather would be upset, and I really didn't want to hurt her feelings, but I had to.

At five thirty, Heather called.

"Hi. How was work today?" I said.

"Not so bad, boring really."

"Can you come over?" I asked.

"Sure. What time?" she replied.

"How about in an hour?" I said.

"Okay."

This was going to be it. I was going to end it that night and hoped my predicament would be over. I kept rehearsing different lines. I wanted to spare her feelings, but my words sounded cruel. I made a pot of coffee and tried to get rid of my buzz, but I was pretty high. I called Big Mike to ask for suggestions, but he wasn't any help. He was really cruel when it came to dumping women. When Heather showed up, I was in the middle of vacuuming my living room, just out of nervousness. She looked great. She had changed her clothes after work and was wearing a hot little dress. She also had makeup on, which was unusual for her.

"The place looks great," she said.

"I clean once a year, whether it needs it or not," I said. "Do you want some coffee or soda?"

"How about a glass of wine?" she said.

"Coming right up."

I put some music on. I couldn't take my eyes off her legs and the dress was quite short. I brought out a bottle of wine and a bag of pot, in case she wanted to smoke. I was thinking now that I would fuck her first, then break up with her, which I realized was really cruel. I couldn't do that. I had to stick to my original plan.

"Do you want to smoke a little?" I said.

"Just a couple of hits," she said.

I loaded up the bond, and we smoked for a few minutes.

"Who was that girl you were with?" she asked.

"Oh, just a friend of mine. She's dating a guy I know. She wanted to smoke some pot and look at my new paintings."

"She's beautiful."

"Yeah, my friend is a lucky guy."

"What's his name?" she asked.

"My friend? David."

"I haven't met him yet."

"No, I don't get to see him much. He's busy all the time."

"What's he do?" she said.
"He's a lawyer."
"A lawyer? Wow! What does she do?" she questioned.
"She's a student."
"She looked pretty young."
"You should have come in and introduced yourself," I said.
"I didn't want to bother you," she replied.

I was afraid she knew I was lying. I was a pretty good liar, but not that good. I didn't wait any longer. I reached over and kissed Heather. She responded by opening her mouth and accepting my tongue. I got a hard-on and pushed her down on the couch. Then she surprised me by saying no and sitting back up.

"Not tonight," she said.
"What's the matter?" I asked.
"I'm not in the mood. That's all."

Now I thought she knew I was lying and had decided to not to have anything more to do with me. My hard-on shriveled right up, and I started feeling uncomfortable. We were sitting a good two feet from each other and conversation felt awkward.

"Do you want some more wine?" I asked.
"No, thank you," she said.
"Something's the matter. Why don't you tell me what it is?" I said.
"I feel all you want from me is sex," she said.
"That's ridiculous!" I exclaimed.
"We only talk for a few minutes. Then you're all over me."
"I can't help it," I said. "I find you irresistible."

She was silent for a minute. I could tell she was frustrated.

"All right," I finally said, "I won't attack you anymore, and we'll spend a lot more time talking."

"Thank you," she said.

Then we were silent again for a while, and she burst out laughing.

"You can sit closer to me," she said.

"I don't want to infringe on your space," I said laughing.

She kissed me on the cheek, and the ice was broken.

"Let's do another hit of pot. That'll make you feel better," I said.

"No thanks. That's enough for me."

I turned off the stereo and turned on the TV. We watched part of a movie and stretched out on the couch. My plans for breaking up with her had gone out the window. I liked her and wanted to hold on to her. After the movie, she decided to leave, and we kissed passionately for a few minutes before we said goodbye. I laughed at myself after she left. I couldn't get my hormones under control long enough to break up with her. Now that she was resisting a bit, she was more of a challenge, and I liked it. I smoked some more pot and listened to Miles Davis before going to bed. It had been a frustrating evening, but at least it was still interesting.

Chapter Fourteen

I had a strange dream that night. Linda and I were sitting in the coffee shop, kissing, when Heather walked in. She was completely naked and soaked from the rain. She came over to our table, picked up my coffee, and poured it over my head. Then she started screaming at Linda, who got up and slapped Heather across the face. That's when I woke up. I laughed to myself and went back to sleep.

In the morning, I got up feeling wide awake and took a hit off the bong. I made the coffee and smoked a cigarette. Early morning was such a peaceful time for me; I read the paper and did a bit of writing, listening to music. It was snowing that morning with large, heavy flakes that floated slowly to the ground. Spring was almost here. The temperature during the day was quite a bit warmer than it usually was.

After showering, I walked to the coffee shop, as usual, thinking about what Heather had said the night before. She was such a good fuck that I wanted to keep going out with her. Linda was already having her coffee when I walked in.

"Hi, sweetheart," I said, giving her a kiss.

"Hi yourself, handsome."

"I couldn't call you last night. Mike was over."

"That's all right. I had a lot of work to do."

"Anything I can help with?" I asked.

"Actually, yes. I'm working with this hardcore feminist writer, and I can't figure out a word she's saying."

"Why don't you bring it over tonight, and I'll look at it."

Her hair was pulled back in a ponytail. I looked at the wisps of hair on the nape of her neck. She was so sexy. I thought maybe tonight was the night I would finally fuck her. If I started fucking Linda, I would definitely break up with Heather.

"I got some bad news last night," she said.

"What's that?" I asked.

"My parents are getting divorced."

"You're kidding!" I cried.

"No. My mother called me. She was in tears. My father has been cheating on her."

"I'm sorry to hear that. How long have they been married?" I asked.

"Almost thirty years."

"That's tough. They must be very upset. How are you handling it?" I said.

"Not very well. I never imagined my parents splitting up. Your parents are divorced too, right?" she questioned.

"Yes. They split when I was eight years old, but I don't remember it affecting me in any particular way."

"I guess it's easier to adjust to when you're just a young kid," she said.

"I would never cheat on my wife," I said. "I've seen too much destruction because of it."

"You don't know for sure. You've never been married, and certainly not for thirty years," she said.

Of course, I was thinking about Heather, but this was a slightly different situation. I wasn't married, and I didn't really feel like I was cheating on either of them.

"That's true," I said.

"Have you ever cheated on a girlfriend?" she asked.

"No," I said, lying through my teeth.

"What's the longest relationship you've ever had?" she said.

"Two years. I just got out of it about a year ago."

"What happened?" she asked.

"She was drinking pretty heavily, and I didn't like the way she was yelling at me for no reason. I would get up in the morning, have my coffee, and be reading the paper, when she would come downstairs hungover and just start yelling."

"Good thing you got out of it. A lot of people stay stuck in their relationships."

"You're right."

I was feeling uncomfortable about lying to her, and I knew she felt bad about her parents splitting up. I renewed my vow to break up with Heather. The stress of going out with both of them was too much.

"How long was your relationship with what's-his-name?" I returned.

"Three and a half years, but we split for a few months in the middle of it."

"Why?" I asked.

"He wanted to go out with someone else."

"I'm glad you broke up with him. You didn't get stuck either."

"It was hard breaking up though. I'll tell you that."

"Sure. It's always hard for both people," I said.

I went up to the counter and ordered another latte. The café was starting to fill up, and I said hello to several people. It began to snow. Heavy flakes floated down, covering the streets. When I sat down again, Linda had a big smile on her face.

"What?" I said.

"Nothing."

Half an hour later, we left, and I went home to paint. I noticed that whenever I was with Linda, I felt in love with her, but when I was with Heather, I felt in love with her. Comparing the two drove me crazy. One would be better in one way, the other in another. I walked home through the snow, preoccupied with my own thoughts. I called Lisa as I smoked a joint and got her out of bed.

"Get your ass out of bed," I said.

"I stayed up late last night," she said. "Let me sleep some more."

"Come on now. We've got work to do."

"I'll be over at eleven," she said.

"All right, but by then I'll be done painting."

"So be it. I'll see you later," she said, hanging up.

I called Little Mike. I knew he'd be up.

"Hey, what's up?" he said.

"My cock."

"Did you get laid last night?" he quizzed.

"No. Did you?" I replied.

"Yup."

"Alicia?" I said.

"No, this new chick."

"Has she got a name?"

"Yeah, but I can't remember it."

"Where'd you find her?" I asked.

"At the club."

"Was she drunk?" I said.

"Of course."

"Is she a good fuck?" I said.

"Decent."

"Are you going to fuck her again?" I continued.

"I could, but I doubt it."

"What are you doing? Do you want to come over?" I asked.

"Got any pot?" he said.

"I swear. That's the only reason you love me."

"It's not the only reason, just the main one," he said. "I'll be over in an hour."

"That'll give me time to do a painting."

"Bye," he said.

Nobody made me laugh like Little Mike. He had a deep sense of irony, combined with sarcasm and cynicism that was timed perfectly. I made a pot of coffee and set up my painting materials. I had been studying a book, which taught me how to sketch faces, and I was going to put my new knowledge to work.

I wanted to paint colorful faces between impressionistic and modern styles, between face and mask with a flavor of primitivism, and between abstract and representation. In short, I wanted to paint something different from anything I had ever seen before. I began almost in the middle of the canvas, following the lines of some imaginary face. Afterward, I painted a barn and a tree and an orange sky surrounding a setting sun. It turned out great.

Shortly after I finished, Mike showed up. He was in a partying mood, as usual, so we fired up the bong.

"So now you think you're a great lover, huh?" I said.

"Well, I'm no Italian Stallion like you, but I'm decent," he laughed.

"Those girls see you tickling the guitar strings and they think you can make them go wild."

"Musicians definitely have an advantage. Did you see Linda this morning?" he asked.

"Yes, I did, and she's coming over this evening. I might get lucky."

"It's not luck, brother. It's a skill."

"You're right."

He got out the guitar and played a few of his own songs. I loved his music. He played with intensity and style, a rare combination. I versed him in some deconstructive ideas of mine to inspire him, but he was just a natural; theory didn't mean much to him. Theory can often interfere with good art. It can stifle creativity and deaden the effect. On the other hand, a little philosophy can spice up a relatively boring story. After he played for a while, he put down the guitar and we smoked some more.

"What's happening with you and Alicia? Have you given up on her?" I said.

"I don't know. I haven't talked to her in two weeks, even though she's left me a couple of messages."

"If you don't like her, why don't you just drop her?" I reasoned.

"A guy's got to get laid every once in a while," he said.

"I know what you mean."

"Are you still stuck in your dilemma?" he said.

"Yes. I'm still fucking the one I don't love, and I'm in love with the one I'm not fucking."

"Maybe that'll change tonight," he said.

"I hope so; this is driving me crazy."

"Not literally, though," he laughed.

"No. I don't get manic over women."

I pulled a cigarette from the pack and lit it. There was nothing like a good cigarette when I was high with a good cup of coffee. I never drank when I smoked pot. It got me too fucked up. Mike had a beer once in a while, but for the most part, we just smoked pot. Mike stayed for another hour. Then he had to go home. I was thinking about Linda, so I decided to clean the house. I completely forgot about Lisa, who showed up while I was vacuuming the living room floor.

"You must have a hot date tonight," she said.

"I sure do. It's Linda."

"Maybe you should be sober for this date," she said, as she took a hit off the bong.

"I will be. I'll take a nap before she comes and make some coffee after I get up."

"I like this painting a lot. You're really getting the hang of doing faces," she said.

"Thanks. I like it too."

After Lisa got high, she got on the floor again to do stretching exercises. She was wearing tight jeans, and her panties were sticking out in the back. I stared at her crotch and touched myself when she wasn't looking. I took a hit off the bong and asked her a question I had been wanting to ask her for a long time.

"Do you want to watch me masturbate?" I asked.

"No," she said emphatically.

"Oh, come on. It's not like we're having sex."

"I said no."

"You're no fun. Can I at least take my clothes off?" I suggested.

"You can if you want to."

That got me excited. I stood up and took off my clothes, revealing a big hard-on. I thought maybe she would take her clothes off, as she had when we had gone camping the summer before. She didn't even look at me, but I was sure she had peeked. I stood there naked, playing with my cock, waiting for her while she continued to stretch.

"Take your clothes off," I said.

"No."

"Come on."

"All right."

She took her pants off and her shirt, but left her underwear on.

"Come on. Everything."

"No, this is good."

I wanted to grab her and rip her panties off, but instead, I stood there, cock in my hand, watching her stretch. She had the nicest body. Her panties were very small. Her ass was hanging out, and her nipples were hard. She put her knees up to her head, and I stared at her crotch, her pubic hair surrounding her panties.

"Come on. Everything off," I said.

"All right."

She took her panties off. Her cunt stared at me in the face, and then her bra entered my vision, her pert tits bobbing up and down.

"Why don't you sketch me," she said.

"Why don't we sketch each other," I replied.

"Good idea."

We got on the couches, pads in hands, and began to sketch each other. I couldn't concentrate. I just wanted to fuck her.

"Spread your legs," I said.

She sat on the floor, her knees up and her legs spread. After I outlined her body, I concentrated on her face, though I kept looking at her cunt.

"Can't we fuck after we're done?" I said.

"No, this is strictly business," she laughed.

After I sketched her, I lay back on the couch and began to

masturbate. She didn't say anything, so I continued. I was so excited, but she continued to draw me as if there were nothing unusual going on. Within minutes I came all over myself, and I heard her laugh. It was one of the most exciting sexual experiences I had ever had.

"Feel better?" she said.

"Yeah, that was great."

"Go shower now," she said.

I went into the bathroom with a smile on my face and took a shower. I started singing at the top of my lungs, knowing that she was laughing. When I came out, she was dressed and still working on the sketch.

"I've got to go," she said.

"All right. I'll call you later."

I took a nap and slept for a long time. My dreams were pleasant, but I didn't remember them. I woke up to the phone ringing. It was Big Mike.

"Hey, what's up?" he said.

"I have a date later with Linda, and Lisa watched me masturbate today."

"Big day," he laughed. "Have you got any pot to sell?"

"A little."

"I'll be up in half an hour."

"Okay."

I got dressed and put on a pot of coffee. I took a couple of hits off the bong and looked at my new painting again. I was really happy with it. Big Mike showed up on time, and I sold him a day's worth of pot. We smoked and laughed for a while until he had to leave. All that was on my mind was fucking Linda. I cleaned the house from top to bottom, even going into the bathroom, which I hated to do. I had an early dinner and waited impatiently for her to show up. She arrived on time and looked great as usual.

She was wearing a deep blue sweater, which highlighted her blonde hair, and she was wearing tight jeans, which made her plump ass stick out.

"How are you, sweetheart?" I said.

"I'm fine, but it's been a hectic day. I couldn't get much studying done. I had to run around and do errands."

"Well, we'll get a lot done tonight."

I made a pot of coffee and had her sit at the dining room table. I was pretty clear-headed. The pot had worn off, and I had closed my eyes for a few minutes. We worked for more than two hours, and she accumulated several pages of notes. We were pretty tired afterward, but I was very horny after sitting next to her all that time, and I still wanted to fuck her.

"Thanks. You've been a big help. This stuff is confusing," she said.

"I know. These writers are pretty confused themselves, which doesn't make it any easier. Would you like a glass of wine now? I'm going to smoke a little."

"Sure! A glass of wine would be great."

After I bought her a glass of wine, I turned on the stereo and rolled a joint. We sat close together on the couch and talked intimately. At one point, I put my arm around her and drew her face to mine. She opened her mouth and closed her eyes, accepting my tongue willingly. I pushed her down on the couch, and we stretched out. I had my right leg between hers, and I began rubbing it into her crotch. She moaned and kissed me passionately.

"My arm is stuck," she said.

I moved over and she pulled her arm out. I unzipped my pants and put her hand on my cock. She massaged it for a while, then took her hand away. Not to mistake lust for love, I felt a wave of passion as I had never felt before. I put my hand between her legs and massaged her pussy. Her pants were still on, but I was trying to unbutton them. My cock was so hard, it was bursting. She grabbed it and started jerking it.

Then, suddenly, she said, "I don't want to make love tonight."

"Why not?" I asked.

"I'm not ready."

"Oh, honey, what's wrong? We've known each other for a while."

My cock shriveled right up.

"I don't feel right about it yet. I know I'm frustrating you, but I can't help it."

I rolled off her and grabbed the bong. I put a lot of pot in the bowl and took a huge hit.

"We can still fool around," she said.

"It only frustrates me," I said. "I'll wait until you're ready," I said.

"I want to kiss you," she said.

"No, that's all right. We're done for this evening."

I was upset for a few minutes, but then I calmed down. I never stayed angry for long.

"Maybe I'd better go," she said.

"It's been a long night. I'll see you in the morning," I said.

After she left, I drew a bath and sat in the hot water for a long time. I knew I would get her the next time, but waiting was hard. After I took my bath, I called Heather.

"Hi, Paul, what's up? It's kind of late to be calling."

"Are you in bed yet?" I asked.

"Almost."

"Do you want to come over?" I said.

"Oh, not tonight, sweetheart. I'll talk to you tomorrow."

"Okay, goodnight."

"Goodnight," she said.

If I hadn't been so frustrated by Linda, I would have never called Heather. I went to bed exhausted and fell right to sleep. It had been a long night, but I still felt that Linda and I had gotten closer.

Chapter Fifteen

There were signs of spring the next day. I awakened to the loud sound of birds singing, and the sun was shining. I made a pot of coffee and lit a cigarette. I always made my coffee strong and put just a little milk in it. I wasn't going to smoke any pot until I had done my writing. I had large windows in my flat, and the sun lit up the place nicely.

I thought about the night before. I was getting closer to fucking Linda, and I had almost lost complete interest in Heather. I sat down to write with my cup of coffee and my cigarette. I decided to write a series of poems about the birds surrounding my house. I wrote two poems and then rolled a joint. I loved to spend my early morning high. The house was peaceful, and my jazz playlist sounded great. After a nice hot shower, I got dressed and decided to walk to the coffee shop. I was anxious to see Linda. She was on my mind constantly. Linda wasn't there when I arrived, so I sat down with the newspaper and had my latte. Half an hour later, she showed up.

"Hi, handsome," she said.

"Hey, kiddo, I was just thinking about you."

"All good, I hope."

"Actually, all my thoughts were naughty."

"I like that."

She got a coffee and sat down. Her hair was pulled back, and she wasn't wearing any makeup. I looked at her skin by the nape of her neck, where wisps of hair were curled. I was, in fact, falling in love with her. It wasn't just lust.

"Thanks for the help last night. You were great."

"No problem. Hey, do you want to come over for dinner tonight? I can help you finish your paper."

"Okay. That sounds good."

"How did you sleep last night?" I asked.

"I slept great. I was so exhausted."

"I dreamed about you," I lied.

"Tell me about it," she said.

"Well, we were camping by a lake. The harvest moon was sitting right above the water, and we were fishing. We were in our bathing suits, and our feet were hanging in the water."

"You're making this up," she said.

"No, I swear."

"Okay. Go on," she laughed.

"Suddenly, a great big fish grabbed your bait and started pulling you into the lake. I held you by your other arm and told you to hang on."

"Why didn't I just let go of the pole?" she said.

"It's a dream. You can't argue with a dream."

"Okay. Go on."

"As the fish pulled you in, I grabbed you by your bathing suit and ripped it right off your body."

She laughed so loud that everybody in the coffee shop looked at us.

"The bottoms or the top?" she said.

"Both!" I said.

"Go on."

"Finally, you let go of the pole and swam to shore, completely naked. I helped you out of the water, and we made love right there on the shore."

"What do you think it means?" she laughed.
"That you lust for me," I replied.
"Or that you lust for me."
"Probably both," I said.
"No wonder you're a writer," she said.
"So, do you want to come over tonight?" I asked.
"What are we going to do?" she said.
"Study, of course."
"Then what?" she asked cautiously.
"Make love."
"I told you. I'm not ready yet."
"Then we'll just study."
"Okay," she said.

We talked for a little while longer until she had to go to class. I stuck around for a while to talk to some of the regulars. Then I went home. I figured Lisa was still sleeping, so I called Little Mike.

"Hey, what's up?" I said.
"Absolutely nothing."
"Did you get laid last night?" I said.
"No. Did you?" he replied.
"No, but I'm getting closer. Linda's coming over again tonight."
"She's playing hard to get?" he said.
"No, I don't think so. She's just taking her time."
"What about Heather?" he asked.
"I haven't talked to her in several days. I'll probably call her today."
"You're a dog."
"I know it."

I talked him into coming over. I wanted to have a few laughs. An hour later, he showed up with his new guitar.

"How's the pot situation?" he said.

"I have a little."

"Well, what are we waiting for?" he said.

"I'll clean out the bong," I said.

We smoked for a while, and he played the guitar. It sounded great, as usual. The notes floated by. He would improvise as he played, not sticking to anything written down, knowing what sounded good, and what chords and notes went with each other. Like any other language, music is in motion and cannot be tied down. He would just play, in every sense of the word, and the moment would linger for a while, then disappear.

"Linda will fuck me tonight. I'll bet you five dollars."

"I'll take that bet. She's playing you, my friend."

"She is not. She really likes me."

"I'm kidding. I know she likes you, but she won't fuck you tonight. She's waiting until you fall in love with her."

"I think you're right about that."

"You can wait. It won't kill you," he said.

"I like the challenge."

"Take your clothes off in front of her. See what she does!" he challenged.

"She'll freak."

"Not necessarily. She might get off on it."

"That's not my style. I like to kiss and kiss, rubbing her all over until she can't resist anymore."

"Yeah, that's what I do too."

"I'll sketch her body, and then we'll get into it."

"That'll work."

He played some more, and we continued to smoke. After an hour, he left, and I decided to call Lisa.

"Do you want to paint?" I asked.

"Sure. I'll be over in a little while."

I got a couple of canvases out of the closet and prepared my paints. I was trying to think of something completely different to paint, but it was difficult. I put on a pot of coffee and waited impatiently for Lisa to show up. I looked at the thermometer outside and noticed that it was going to be a pretty warm day. There were dark clouds overhead. It was probably going to rain.

Lisa came over about an hour later, looking great. She had her tight jeans on as usual, and under her coat, she was wearing a small tank top.

"How did it go last night?" she said.

"I'm making progress. She's coming over tonight too."

"She's just about ready?" she asked.

"I think so."

"Then what are you going to do? Find somebody else?" she questioned.

"Oh, come on. I really like her."

"That's what you said about Heather."

"This is different."

"Sure."

Lisa knew me pretty well. I couldn't get anything past her, but I really felt this situation was different. I was in love with Linda, and conquering meant keeping her, I thought.

"What do you want to paint?" Lisa said.

"I think I want to paint your face."

"Really."

"Yeah, I don't know if I can do it, but I'd like to try."

I had her sit on the couch, and I set up my easel a few feet away. I turned on all the lights in the living room since it was so dark out, and then rolled a joint.

"Are you going to do my face in different colors?" she asked.

"I'm not sure yet," I said, lighting the joint. "Do you want to take your clothes off?" I said.

"No."

"Oh, come on."

"Stop right now, Paul, or I won't pose for you."

"All right. All right."

I started painting the wind, not the sky, the wind; different colors flowing through the sky, moving in different directions. Then I went to her face. I began with the eyes and worked my way around, using the same colors as before. Soon, I was done, but it didn't look like her.

"Oh well, it doesn't resemble you," I said.

"Let me see," she said. "Oh, it's great though."

"Yeah, I kind of like it too."

"There must be hundreds of different colors there."

"It's your turn."

"What should I paint?" she said.

"Why don't you paint an artist at work?" I offered.

"That's a good idea. Do you want to sit for me?" she said.

"No. Do it from your imagination. It'll turn out better."

She painted for half an hour while I drank coffee and smoked. She was borrowing techniques from me, and her colors were brilliant. When she was done, she stepped back and took a close look.

"Wow!" I said.

"Oh, I'm so happy," she said.

"You're really getting the hang of this," I said.

"Thanks to you."

"Don't give me any credit. You did this on your own," I said.

"But doing it with you makes it so much easier."

I gave her a big hug and a kiss on the lips. I felt a wave of love flow over me and wished she were mine. What a team we would make, I thought. A little while later, she had to leave, and I gave her another kiss, this time on the cheek.

"Bye, sweetheart. I'll call you later," I said.

I took a long nap and thought about my coming evening with Linda. When I got up, I cleaned the house from top to bottom, even the bathroom. I went out to get some groceries and a bottle of wine. The weather had changed; dark clouds had invaded the sky, and there was a light rain.

Right at six o'clock, she showed up, looking great. I had candles lit on the dining room table. The atmosphere was very sensuous.

"I thought we were going to study!" she said immediately.

"We are, we are. Relax. Are you hungry?" I asked.

"Yes. A little."

"Come on. I've got some shrimp and scallops, and your favorite wine."

"I can't drink wine before I study."

"Just a glass. We'll finish the rest later."

I took her knapsack and coat and sat her down at the table. I poured a glass of wine for each of us and went to the kitchen.

"It'll be ready in a minute," I said.

"Is this your new painting?" she asked.

"The one on the right," I said.

"They're both great. The one of that Lisa chick is coming right along. I'm jealous."

"I can teach you how to paint, too, if you want."

"I'm too busy right now, maybe this summer."

I finished cooking and served us at the table.

"Wow! This looks great."

"It's easy. Just sauté the seafood in butter and wine."

"You'd make somebody a good wife someday," she said.

After eating, we cleared the table, and she pulled out her books. I read what she had written so far and made suggestions. After a couple of hours, we quit, and I poured us a glass of wine each.

"Thanks, Paul. You've been a big help."

"My pleasure, sweetheart."

I took out the bong and put the bowl in it. I took a big hit and loaded it for her. She took a hit and coughed so hard I thought she was going to fall over.

"Easy, girl, you're just not used to it."

I thought if I could get her fucked up, I could get her pants off. We each took a few more hits and then stopped.

"You're trying to take advantage of me," she said.

"Of course I am. Can I sketch you?" I asked.

"That sounds like fun."

"But you have to take your clothes off."

"Okay."

I was surprised she was so willing. She took her clothes off and sat on the floor with her legs spread. I got a hard-on immediately. She had a big smile on her face and couldn't stop talking while I sketched. I finished in ten minutes. All I wanted to do was fuck her. I motioned for her to sit on the couch next to me, and she came right over. I stood up and took my clothes off. My cock was as hard as a rock. She leaned over and put my cock in her mouth. This was the first real sexual contact we had had.

I wanted to wait until I fucked her, but I came in her mouth. She gagged on it a little, which made me laugh. We kissed for a long time, and I licked her pussy until she came. After half an hour, I got hard again and put my cock in her cunt. She was tight, very tight, and it felt great.

"Take it slow for a while," she said.

I felt such a strong emotion toward her. I had wanted her for so long. Now, I was definitely in love. As I kissed her, I fucked her slowly for a long time. She moaned with her eyes closed as I increased my speed.

"I love you," I said.

"I love you too."

That's what I had wanted to hear. I thrust harder and harder until I was ready to come. Then I pulled out. I came on her stomach and fell exhausted into her arms.

"You took advantage of me," she teased.

"You took advantage of me," I said.

I thought about how much more intense the lovemaking was with Linda than with Heather. I was down to one girlfriend, which was where I had wanted to be from the beginning.

"You're a good fuck," she said.

"So are you."

"Can I spend the night?" she asked.

"Of course."

"Let's take a shower," I suggested.

"Good idea," she said.

We got in the shower and soaped each other. I got hard again and turned her to face the wall. I put my cock inside her while reaching around and rubbing her clit.

"You're driving me wild!" she said.

I couldn't come this time, but I stayed hard a long time. After the shower, we went into the living room to watch TV. I smoked some pot while she sipped on a glass of wine. We went to bed completely satisfied and slept very well.

Chapter Sixteen

In the morning, I woke up feeling rested with a smile on my face. I went into the bathroom while she was still sleeping and brushed my teeth. I had a hard-on as I got back into bed. I put my hand between her legs and rubbed her gently until she awakened.

"Good morning, sweetheart," I said.

"Oh, that feels good; keep doing it," she said.

I pulled the covers down and licked her pussy. In two minutes, she came. She sucked on my cock for a while until I came. What a way to wake up! We got in the shower and fucked our brains out.

"I could get used to this," she said.

"Me too."

We both wanted to go back to bed, but she had things to do. I cooked a quick breakfast, and she was gone in half an hour. I decided to do some writing, but I could hardly concentrate, so I gave up. I smoked a joint and called Little Mike.

"Hey, what's up?" I said, all excited.

"What are you so happy about?" he demanded.

"Linda and I finally did it last night and this morning."

"Congratulations. Now let me go back to sleep."

All right. I'll call you later."

I knew Lisa would still be sleeping, so I didn't call her. I decided to go to the coffee shop to see who was hanging out. I was there for a little while but didn't see any of the regulars. They had already gone to work or school. I sat there, sipping my latte, thinking about Linda, and rejoicing in my good fortune. I fantasized about what we would do in bed the next time we got together and had her in all kinds of positions.

When I returned home, I decided it was a safe time to call Lisa.

"Are you up?" I said.

"Yeah, I've been up for an hour."

"I got lucky last night."

"Did you?" she asked.

"We had a great time, definitely one of the best nights of my life."

"Well, good for you."

"Do you want to come over?" I said.

"For a little while, I guess."

"See you soon," I said.

I was hoping that Lisa would have been jealous, even a bit, but I didn't detect anything in her voice. I looked outside. It was beginning to rain, another dark day in Syracuse. I prepared one of my canvases but had no idea what I was going to paint. Lisa showed up later, so I cleaned out the bong. She was wearing her jeans with holes in the knees, which I found very sexy.

"What are we going to paint today?" she said.

"I don't know. I don't even really feel like painting."

"Do you want to hang out?" she said.

"I thought maybe I could sketch you again," I said.

"Naked?" she asked.

"Why not?" I pressed.

"You're a horny dude, aren't you?" she said.

"No different from anyone else."

"Let's just smoke and talk. How about that?" she said.

"Okay."

I filled up the bowl and passed the bong to her. Then I heard the doorbell ring.

"I wonder who that could be?" I said.

It was Little Mike.

"Hey, what are you guys up to?" he said.

"Just smoking, come on in," I said.

"So you had a great night last night," Mike said.

"I'm definitely in love."

"Yeah, I've heard that before," Lisa said.

"This time it's for real. I'm going to marry this woman."

I thought about the wedding day and honeymoon for a split second, and a smile came over my face.

"Let me at least enjoy my fantasy," I said.

"No. I think it's great. Maybe this is the one," Mike said.

"Of course, it's great," Lisa said, though I detected a note of sarcasm.

I figured they were both jealous because neither of them was in love. I felt good, and I wasn't going to let anyone affect that feeling. I lit a cigarette and gave one to Mike, who only smoked cigarettes when he was smoking pot, which was most of the time. Lisa took another hit off the bong, and I could tell she was really high.

"There's nothing like an early morning high," Mike said.

"What are you going to say to Heather now?" Lisa said.

"I don't know. I'll think of something."

"This thing with Linda isn't a sure thing yet. Maybe you'd better hold off," Mike said.

"No, my relationship with Heather has run its course. There's nothing left."

"You men are impossible," Lisa said.

"Why?" I said.

"You think you're a player," she said.

"I'm not a player," I said. "This is the first time I was going out with two women, and I had to make a decision. What's wrong with that?"

"You don't even care about hurting Heather's feelings," she said.

"I do too care about hurting her feelings. Why do you think I've been putting it off for so long?" I said, getting slightly irritated.

"You're insincere," she said.

"I'm no different than anyone else," I said.

She had hurt my feelings, and I wasn't sure how to react to it. I figured I probably deserved it, but it made me angry. Mike was on my side. He knew how men acted and how they felt, but more importantly, he felt guilty too and identified with me.

"What about you?" I said to Lisa.

"What about me?" she spoke.

"You're taking advantage of Jason. He loves you, but it's not requited."

"I love him in my own way."

"Sure."

"All right you two. Cut it out," Mike said. "You're ruining my high."

I stopped talking, but I was still angry. Lisa walked over to me and gave me a kiss on the cheek. We hung around for another hour. Then they left. I was still pissed at Lisa, but all I could think about was Linda. She was going to be in class all day, but we had made plans to get together that evening.

I decided to call Big Mike to see what he was doing.

"Hey," I said.

"What's up with you, bro?" he said.

"Linda and I finally got together last night."

"Hey, that's great. What are you going to tell Heather?" he asked.

"Everybody keeps asking me that. How the hell should I know?" I snapped.

"Easy, easy. What's got you so upset?" he said.

"I'm sorry. Lisa was giving me a bit of a hard time, but she apologized, sort of."

"About Heather?" he questioned.

"Yes."

"Hey, listen. We all take our chances when we go out with somebody. Heather will get over it."

"I know, but I still feel bad. I really like her."

I thought about my eventual conversation with Heather, and I imagined how she would react. Maybe she would yell at me, which would bother me greatly, or maybe she would be silent. Either way, it would hurt both of us. We were deeply fond of each other, and she had helped me through some tough times.

"Heather is a mature woman. She knows what it's like to lose a man," he said.

"It still doesn't hurt any less," I said.

"Are you sure you want to break up with her now? You'll never be able to go back to her."

"That's what Little Mike said. I think it's time."

I imagined Linda breaking up with me right after I dumped Heather. What a shock that would be! Linda said she was in love though. I couldn't see her breaking up with me at this stage.

"Hey, do you want to come up for a while this afternoon?" I asked Mike.

"Sure, I'll come up. What's the pot situation?" he replied.

"I've got some."

"See you later," he said.

After I hung up the phone, I decided to take a nap. I curled up with my cat and fell right to sleep. Half an hour later, my eyes popped open. I felt refreshed and ready to smoke again. I rolled a joint and put on some jazz. I loved all this free time and thought back to when I had been in a relationship with Laura and had had very little time to myself.

A few hours later, Big Mike showed up with a putter and some golf balls. He was addicted to golf and wanted to practice putting in my living room.

I thought back to the previous summer, when I had played golf with Lisa. It was her first time on a course, and she was having a lot of trouble. I showed her how to hold the club and from behind her, I reached around to show her the swing. I held her close as she pulled back the club, keeping it on plane and stopping when the club was parallel with the ground. She was very limber and a quick learner. I watched her as she swung the club, an intensity in her face and a vicious hip rotation. She didn't score very well, but we had a lot of fun, and I was looking forward to playing with her again the next summer.

I put on some music and cleaned out the bong. We cleared an area in the living room to putt and put a glass at one end.

"What did Lisa say to you that made you so angry?" Mike asked.

"She thinks I was playing Heather and using her for my own purposes."

"I don't think you were using Heather. It was just bad timing for her. If you hadn't met Linda, you two would have been very happy."

"I still can't help feeling guilty, but Lisa knows me better than that."

"Maybe Lisa is jealous."

"I thought of that, but I don't think so."

"You never know what a woman is thinking. You have to read between the lines."

Big Mike was a good putter and could concentrate on his golf while he was talking. I, on the other hand, was missing putt after putt, thinking about what was happening in my personal life.

"Maybe you shouldn't say anything to Heather; just let it fade into the background."

"No, I can't do that. I at least owe her an explanation."

I kept rehearsing a speech in my head for Heather, but it didn't sound too great. I tried making up a big lie, but that didn't seem right either. It was going to be very difficult. There was no way around it, and I was dreading it.

"Tell her you're seeing someone else. She'll understand," he said.

"That's what I'm going to tell her. I'm just scared. That's all."

"You guys haven't been going out for very long. You're not going to hurt her too badly."

"I guess you're right."

I kept thinking about what Lisa had said to me. I didn't realize quite how much she had hurt me. I also thought about seeing Linda later in the day, and that made me feel better. Mike and I hung out for another hour or so before he left to do some work. I was left alone with my own thoughts, so I smoked some more pot and floated out into the world of unreality. My addiction to pot was getting more severe without me even realizing it. Eventually, I would have to do something about it, but at that time, I simply did it without caring.

Chapter Seventeen

A couple of hours later, I got a phone call. It was Heather.

"Hi, sweetie. How are you?" she said.

"I'm fine. I'm sorry I haven't called you. I've been busy," I said.

"It's all right. I've been busy too. I miss you."

"I miss you too."

"So, how's the painting going?" she asked.

"Fine, fine."

"And the writing?" she continued.

"Actually, I've been concentrating on the painting lately."

"Why don't we get together soon," she said.

"Sure. How about Saturday night?" I suggested.

"That's great. What time?" she said.

"Eight o'clock."

"I'll be there," she said.

I simply couldn't do it. I had wanted to say something, but the words wouldn't come out. Now I was stuck with going out with Heather at least one more time, while all my affections were directed toward Linda. I figured I could call Heather back, but then I thought I would break up with her in person on Saturday night.

I cleaned the house and smoked some more pot. I didn't care about being straight for Linda; she was used to seeing me high. I had plenty of food and a bottle of wine, so I was prepared. At six o'clock sharp, she arrived.

"Hey, what's up, kid?" I said.

"I thought about you all day today. I couldn't even concentrate on my classes."

"A gentleman has that effect on a lady."

"Did you paint today?" she asked.

"No. I took the day off."

"Do you realize people would kill to be in your situation?" she said.

"I do have it pretty good."

"The whole house smells like pot. You might want to get an air filter."

"Good idea. Do you want to smoke?" I offered.

"No, but I'll have a glass of wine."

"Coming right up."

I wondered if it bothered her that I got high so much, but I certainly wasn't going to quit if it did. I opened the bottle of wine and poured us both a glass.

"I thought about you all day, too," I said.

"What were you thinking?" she asked.

"How much in love with you I am."

"That's what I was thinking."

"We make a good team."

I put on some Miles Davis and reveled in the music. After she finished her glass of wine, she had a big smile on her face.

"Let's make love," I said.

"Not yet. You have to have a little anticipation. Let's talk first."

"What do you want to talk about?" I asked.

"I don't know. Anything."

"I certainly don't want to talk about anything intellectual."

"Why not?" she said.

"I've had enough of that."

I realized I was being too anxious and decided to pull back. We always had things to talk about, but I really wanted to jump into bed. She was so sexy I couldn't resist her. That was the first moment I thought, perhaps, I wasn't in love but merely motivated by the sex. I dismissed the thought and calmed down.

"I'm kidding," I said. "Let's talk about whatever you want to talk about."

"It's a two-way street. Don't you want to talk?" she asked.

"Of course I do."

"Did you hear about the bombing in the Middle East?" she said.

"No. I didn't watch the news today. What happened?" I said.

"You're not interested."

"No, I am. Tell me."

"Well then, let's talk about us."

"What about us?" I said. "I've found that if you let the relationship develop without analyzing it all the time, it works better. When a problem arises, then we'll talk about it."

"Why are you being like this?" she said.

"Like what?" I protested.

"Like that!"

"I'm sorry. I guess I'm being a real pain in the ass," I said.

"Yes, you are."

"I've had a bad day. It's not really you."

"Well then, let's talk about it. Why did you have a bad day?" she said.

"I don't want to talk about it," I said.

I knew right at that moment that we weren't going to have sex that evening. I kept staring at her crotch. I wanted to get laid in the worst way.

"Why don't you want to talk about it? It's not healthy to bottle up everything inside," she said.

"Can't we just skip it? Let's talk about your research," I said.

"I thought you didn't want to talk about anything intellectual? Besides, I'd rather talk about what's bothering you."

"Forget it."

"All right. I won't push it," she said.

We sat there in silence for a long time. I wanted to kiss her, but I was in a bad mood, and I knew she was too.

Finally, I said, "Do you want to spend the night?"

"No. I'm going home. We'll try again tomorrow."

"I'm sorry."

"Don't worry about it. Things like this happen."

After she left, I was even more upset. All I had to do was talk to her, but how could I have told her about Heather? I smoked some more pot, my answer to everything, and I felt better. The next day, I would have to really apologize to her. I was grateful she had taken it so well. I went to bed tired and frustrated, but fell right to sleep.

Fortunately, everything looks better in the morning. I got up feeling cheerful and excited about the day, which was my normal way of waking up. I made some coffee and lit a cigarette. I decided to wait several hours before smoking pot.

It was raining out, and the wind was blowing. All the snow had melted. I had a speech all organized for Linda. I was going to apologize and get her to come over that night. I did some writing and got on my exercise cycle for a few minutes, which I rarely did. I was feeling great, so I decided not to smoke until after going to the coffee shop.

I got to the coffee shop early, but no one was there yet, so I talked to the girl behind the counter. I wanted to get high in the worst way. I always had my pot on me, in case of emergencies, so I went out to my car and rolled a joint. The girl who worked at the coffee shop saw me and decided to join me. We smoked a joint together, and I flirted with her for a couple of minutes until she had to go back to work. Now I was high, and I didn't want to talk to Linda in that condition, so I drove home.

Smoking pot was becoming a problem. It was controlling me instead of the other way around, and it bothered me. I wanted to quit but didn't know how to go about it. When I stopped, I craved it and ended up going back to it. I was spending more and more time alone. I rarely went out, and I avoided people I knew.

I called Little Mike when I got home. He was up and wanted to get high, so I invited him over. A few minutes later, he showed up at my doorstep.

"Hey, what's up?" he said.

"Nothing."

"What's the matter?" he asked.

"Oh, nothing. I was going to talk to Linda, but then I got high, so I came home. This pot thing is out of control"

"Maybe you should quit."

"How can I quit? All my friends smoke. It's part of my everyday routine."

"Yeah, that's a tough one."

I automatically pulled out the bong and filled up the bowl. We smoked for a while, and I felt better.

"Smoking a little pot isn't that bad," he said.

"A little? Do you know how much this costs me every day? Forty bucks!" I exclaimed.

"You can afford it."

"Barely. Besides, that's not the point. I don't want to avoid Linda."

"She knows you smoke."

"Yes, but I don't think she's too crazy about it."

"I'll help you quit. I won't smoke over here, and we'll get the others to join in."

"It won't work."

I thought about Linda and how fucked up the situation was. I looked out at the dreary rain and felt like escaping to California.

"Maybe you should go into rehab," he said.

"I thought of that."

"And?" he pressed.

"Well, I will if I have to, but what guarantee is there that it'll work?" I replied.

"There's never a guarantee, but it's a start."

"Why don't you quit with me?" I said.

"I'm not ready to quit yet," he said.

"See what I mean? I'm not ready to give up my friends."

"You don't have to give us up. Why don't you cut back and smoke in the evenings or every three days?" he suggested.

"I tried that, but I crave it in the worst way. I'm going to have to quit completely."

"If you're determined," he said, "you can do it. I know you can."

"Thanks for the vote of confidence," I said.

We were high, so it was relatively easy to talk about quitting. It would be more difficult in the morning when it was time to abstain.

Chapter Eighteen

Mike and I listened to music for the rest of the day and lay around like vegetables. I was not happy. The effects of the pot were not the same as when I had begun several years earlier. I only felt euphoric in the morning for a number of hours. Then I stayed numb.

In the evening, I called Lisa to see what she was up to.

"Did you paint today?" she asked.

"No. Mike and I just hung out."

"I didn't get much done today either," she said.

"I've got to quit getting high. It's making my life impossible."

"I didn't realize you were having such a problem with it."

"I completely avoided Linda today, and there are all kinds of other things that I'm prevented from doing."

"I know what you mean."

"Do you want to quit too?" I asked.

"Not really."

"Great."

"Well, why should I quit because you have a problem with it?" she said.

"I don't know. I was hoping my friends would quit with me."

"That's not very realistic. What did Mike say?" she asked.

"Same thing you did."

I was getting frustrated, and, for the first time, I realized I would have to go to a rehab center and give up my old friends.

This was a daunting prospect, and I wasn't looking forward to it.

"I think I have to go to rehab," I said.

"You can't quit on your own?" she said.

"I don't think so, and I'm going to have to distance myself from you guys."

"You're kidding."

"Does it sound like I'm kidding?" I said.

"Paul!" she exclaimed.

"There's no other way. I'm sick of being high all the time. Linda and I will be new best friends."

"That hurts my feelings."

"I'm sorry, but that's how it has to be."

I didn't really know if I could carry it all out or not, but I really was sick of it all. I didn't want to hurt Lisa's feelings, but nobody else wanted to quit with me, so I would have to quit them. After I talked to Lisa, I called my mother.

"Hi, Ma."

"Hi, kid," she said.

"Listen, Mom, I have to go to rehab."

"For pot? I didn't know you had to."

"I'm addicted."

"All right. We can do that. Do you know of a rehab center around here?" she said.

"I don't want to go here," I said.

"Where do you want to go?" she asked.

"I've heard of a really good one in southern California."

"Sounds expensive. You don't have any medical insurance."

"I know, but I have to go."

"I understand. I'll pay for it."

"I'm going to call them today."

"Fine. Let me know."

After I hung up, I felt a great burden lifted off my shoulders. I called Linda immediately.

"Hi. I missed you at the coffee shop," she said.

"I know. I had some business to take care of. I'm going to a rehab center. I have to stop smoking pot. It's out of control."

"That's great! I'm so proud of you. That takes a lot of courage."

I felt relieved she responded that way. I was worried, I guess, unnecessarily, that she would be upset. I needed her support since she was my only friend who didn't smoke.

"What rehab are you going to?" she asked.

"It's in California. That's the only thing. You're not going to be able to visit me."

"How long are you going for?" she asked.

"Probably six months."

"Ouch! That's a long time, but I'll be waiting for you when you come back."

"Thanks. I'm counting on it."

I thought she probably wouldn't be waiting for me after such a long time, but it was possible.

"I'll call you as often as I can," I said.

"I'll write you," she said.

"Why don't you come over tonight?" I asked.

"All right."

After I hung up with her, I called information to get the number for the rehab center. I got in touch with them right away and made arrangements to be there in three days. I called my mother and let her book my flight. I was getting excited. I hadn't been to southern California in a long time and I was really looking forward to it. It might sound strange to be looking forward to going to rehab, but that's how I felt.

Linda came over a little while later. She gave me a big hug and kissed me passionately.

"I'm leaving in three days," I said.

"I'm going to miss you so much," she said.

"I have to do this."

"I know."

I poured her a glass of wine and rolled a joint.

"What kind of place is it?" she asked.

"They do intensive work in groups. They're close to the beach, so you feel like you're on vacation. At least, that's what I've heard. We'll see."

"I hope it doesn't turn into a nightmare."

"No. It really has a good reputation."

"Maybe I can come out there to visit you after the semester."

"That would be great."

"You'd better not hook up with one of those beach bunnies."

"I won't. I'm there for one reason only; besides, I love you."

I kissed her and pushed her down on the couch. She unbuttoned my shirt as I thrust up against her. I figured this might be my last time to make love for several months, so I was going to make the best of it. We didn't talk during my lovemaking, but it was very passionate. We kissed a lot, and I came inside her mouth. She swallowed it right down and smiled.

"I love you," she said.

"I can't tell you how much I love you," I said.

We took a shower together, and I massaged her back.

"What am I going to do without you?" she said.

"Just don't find somebody else to go out with," I said.

"I won't even talk to anybody else," she said. "Besides, I have too much work to do."

"You can ask me questions over the phone, and I'll try to

help you."

"I'll send you a couple of papers, and you can mark them up."

"It would be great if you could visit me."

"I'll try; I really will."

For a moment, I imagined the beach in California, the waves lapping gently against the sand. I needed sunshine and lots of it. I knew there would be strong Santa Ana winds, but there wouldn't be any rain. The air would be clean, and I wouldn't be high.

"Have you ever been to California?" I asked.

"No. That's one reason I want to go so badly."

"It's beautiful, really spectacular."

"Maybe we could stay there for a while after you get out."

"You have to come back to school."

"I can take some time off."

"It would be like a honeymoon," I said.

She was silent for a few seconds, seriously pondering what I had just said.

"Don't tease me about that," she said.

"I'm not. I think we should get married."

"I couldn't believe I had said it, but I didn't regret it.

"Not yet," she said.

"Of course," I said, feeling let down.

"You've got to quit smoking pot first."

"I'm going to. I promise."

"We'll see. I'll keep it in mind."

I wanted to make love to her again, but thought better of it. I was optimistic that she really would marry me if I quit smoking, and it was a great incentive. She didn't spend the night, and it took me longer than usual to fall asleep. I had so much on my mind. When I finally did fall asleep, I had strange, violent dreams that kept waking me in the night.

I got out of bed early in the morning; I was tired of dreaming. I made a very strong pot of coffee and rolled a joint. I didn't want to get high, but had to. I smoked the joint and wrote a poem about leaving home. Everyone I knew was still sleeping, so I chilled out and listened to music. When the coffee shop opened, I left the house. I had to get out of the house. The young girl named Janet was working when I arrived.

"You're up early," she said.

"I always get up early."

"What'll you have?" she asked.

"A double latte, please."

"It's going to rain all day," she said.

"Figures. I'm so sick of this Syracuse weather."

"Me too. I'm moving to Florida or California when I'm done with school."

"I'm going to California in a couple of days," I said.

"For good?" she replied.

"I don't know, maybe."

"Really? Just pick up and go?" she said.

"Sort of."

"Don't you own a house here, Paul?" she asked.

"Yeah, but we can always sell that."

"Take me with you," she said.

"You can go by yourself," I said. "You're young; you don't have any attachments here."

"I'd like to. I really would."

I was tired of talking to her already. I only wanted to sit quietly and make my plans. I figured Linda would be in within the next hour, so I sat down and read the newspaper. I looked out at the dreary weather and felt excited again about going to California. Half an hour later, Linda showed up. I was so glad to see her.

"Hi. How do you feel this morning?" she said.

"What do you mean?" I said.

"Are you still excited about going to California?" she asked.

"Yes, I'm thrilled."

"Good."

"The more I think about it, the more I think I might just stay out there. I feel better in the sunshine."

"I know what you mean. This weather is really getting to me. As I was walking in, a gust of wind picked up and pelted me right in the face with the rain."

"Why don't you transfer to UCLA or USC and finish your studies in California?" I suggested.

"I'll have to think about that," she said.

I didn't want to leave her behind; I really didn't. I was afraid I would never see her again. But I had to go to California. I had made my decision, and I was sticking to it. I would come back, if I had to, and try to revive our fledgling relationship.

"Are you really thinking about staying in California?" she said.

"Yes, I really am."

"That's a big move."

"Why don't you come with me? I've got some money. We can start a new life out there."

"It's so far away from my family," she said.

"I can be your new family."

"What about you? Can you stand to be so far away from your mother and your brother?" she said.

"If I'm with you, I can; it's only a plane flight away," I said.

"Yes, but it's the difference between seeing our families once a year, or on a regular basis."

She was right, of course, and I knew it. I would never get away from the Syracuse weather. I would end up going out there for a few months and coming back.

"I'm worried about losing you," I said.

"You won't lose me," she smiled tenderly.

Chapter Nineteen

"I have to go home and pack," I said to Linda.

"Okay," she said. "I'll see you later."

I went home and rolled another joint. I was getting nervous about leaving. I wanted to call Lisa but decided I would leave my friends alone for the day. Then I changed my mind and called her.

"Hey, what's up?" she said.

"I'm packing today."

"Want some help?" she said.

"Sure."

"I'll be over in a little while."

When she arrived, I was sitting comfortably in front of the television, not worried about a thing. I got up and let her in. I was glad to see her. I couldn't imagine giving her up.

"You haven't packed a thing," she said.

"I'm in no hurry. I have a few days."

"Is this the last day we're going to see each other?"

"I don't know, Lisa. What do you want me to tell you? You're my best friend. I think we can hang out on a limited basis when I get back, but you can't smoke pot in front of me."

"I won't, I promise. I might even quit myself."

"Do you mean it? That would be great."

While we were talking, I was packing the bong. I was going to get high until the minute I stepped on the plane.

"What's going on with you and Linda?" she asked.

"We're in love. She might visit me in California."

"Do you think you should give Heather a call?" she said.

"I think I'm just going to disappear into the sunset."

"That might be the best way to handle it. She'll get over it."

"How does Linda feel about you going to rehab?" she asked.

"She's thrilled. She's all in favor of it."

"I'm thrilled too; you have incredible potential; I can't wait to see what you can do clean and sober."

After we got high, Lisa and I went into my bedroom, and I dragged out two suitcases.

"How long do you think you'll stay out there?" Lisa said.

"I'm planning on going for six months," I said.

I guess two big suitcases will be enough. You can buy stuff out there if you need more," she said.

She folded my shirts while I packed my summer clothes. I had been watching the weather channel to see what the temperature was like out there. As I packed my clothes, I was getting excited. If I could, I would turn this into a vacation.

"Are you going to call me and write me once you get out there?" Lisa said.

"Of course."

"I'm going to really miss you," she said.

It didn't take us long to pack. I decided to take a few manuscripts with me and some paintings. I don't know why. After packing, we listened to music until she had to leave. I didn't quite know what to do with myself, so I cleaned out the bong and took several hits. I called Little Mike, who was getting up at the time.

"Hey, what's up?" he said.

"I'm packing for rehab.

"California, here you come," he said.

"Yeah, but it'll probably be a pain in the ass."

"You never know; you might have fun."

"It'll be all right, I guess."

"Sure! You'll meet a babe or two out there."

"I'm trying to be faithful to Linda. She might come out to visit me."

"Whatever. I know you. You'll be fucking somebody out there."

"I don't think so."

"When you quit smoking, you'll be hornier than a dog in heat."

"Maybe, but if I do fuck somebody, it won't affect how I feel about Linda."

"You're really serious about Linda. That's good. Can I be the godfather of your first child?" he joked.

"Sure. Do you want to come over?" I said.

"Yeah, I'll be over in an hour," he said.

After I hung up, I decided to clean the apartment, so that when I returned it would look good. I vacuumed and mopped the kitchen floor. Then I smoked more pot. When Mike came over, we smoked a bit and put on Miles Davis. He played along on his guitar, and I thought I had better enjoy this high because I would have to quit in a day or so.

"So are you going to avoid me after you quit smoking?" he said.

"That's exactly what Lisa said," I answered.

"What did you tell her?" he said.

"I said that as long as you guys don't smoke around me, I can see you once in a while.

"Great."

"I'm sorry, but that's the way it has to be. You're still my best friends."

"I should quit too," he said.

"It's not that easy," I said.

"I don't want to go to rehab, but I think I can quit on my own."

"Try it. See how it works out. I think you'll be glad that you did," I said.

I had tried many times to quit on my own, but, obviously, it had not worked. I would have to get into an outpatient program, and then join a support group, all of which I had planned out.

"I like to smoke when I play music though. That's my only problem," he said.

"There are millions of people who play music and don't get high," I said.

"I know. It's probably only an excuse."

"You and Lisa can quit together, and the three of us will find other things to do," I said.

"That sounds good. I'm getting pretty sick of this myself."

We hung out for another hour or so. Then he took off. I called Linda and talked to her for a while; she agreed to come over later that day. I took a long nap and dreamt of California.

At five o'clock, Linda showed up wearing tight jeans and a bright sweater. Her hair was pulled back in a ponytail, and she looked great.

"What's up, girl?" I said.

"I was thinking how much I'm going to miss coming over here and hanging out," she said.

"I'll be back soon. I'm starting to think that maybe I'll go out there for only three months."

"Will that be long enough?" she asked.

"I think so."

I didn't wait any longer. I leaned over and started kissing her. She moaned and opened her mouth wide. I pushed her back on the couch and put my hand down her pants. She was so wet.

"Let's go to the bedroom," she said.

We took our clothes off quickly and dove into bed. I licked her pussy until she came. She arched her back and held my head between her legs. I had juice all over my face. Then she sucked on me for a long time, slowly and lovingly. Before I came, I stopped her and crawled on top of her. I was so hard, and the head of my cock was large and purple. I started fucking her slowly, taking my time, until finally, I thrust really hard and came inside her.

"I want to have a baby with you," I said.

"I do too," she said.

"You do?"

"Yes."

I kissed her passionately and squeezed her as hard as I could.

"I love you," I said.

"I love you too," she said.

We took a shower and got dressed. I rolled a joint and smoked it while she drank a glass of wine.

"When are you taking off?" she said.

"Day after tomorrow, early."

"I'm going to be really busy tomorrow. So this has to be our goodbye."

We talked for a long time, mostly about California. She was planning to come out after the semester. When I said goodbye to her that evening, I almost had tears in my eyes. I had a lot of trouble sleeping the next two nights, even though I had smoked a lot of pot.

Chapter Twenty

Two days later, I was up early, getting ready for my flight. My mother was coming to take me to the airport. I smoked three joints, figuring it would last me at least until I got to Chicago, but I didn't bring any pot with me. I was already completely packed, so all I had to do was shave and shower. My mother, of course, was right on time, and I stumbled down the steps as I left the house.

"How do you feel?" she asked.

"Fine. Right now, I'm high as hell."

"Are you going to be able to make your connection in that kind of shape?" she asked.

"Sure. I have two hours in Chicago."

My mother didn't understand anything about drug abuse or alcoholism. She knew that in my twenties, when I was in college and graduate school, I hardly touched a thing. Now, things were different. I wanted to get back to clean living, when I didn't need anything artificial to feel good.

I got on the flight as scheduled and slept all the way to Chicago. When we arrived, I was perfectly straight. I ate a slice of pizza and smoked a few cigarettes in Chicago, then boarded my flight for LA. There would be a van waiting for me at LAX to take me north to the rehab center. At around five o'clock that evening, I got to the center safe and sound. I had seen the beautiful houses in Malibu, and the drive along Route 1 was spectacular. I ate dinner and joined the others in the television room. I wanted to call Linda, but they said I wouldn't have phone privileges for several days. I went to sleep early, very tired, but I couldn't sleep without the help of the pot.

I went outside several times during the night to smoke and to talk to the night staff. There was one guy, Andre, who I would become good friends with. He worked at night and had a great sense of humor.

The accommodation was very nice. There was carpeting throughout, and I had a great room by myself. I shared a bathroom with a sex addict. The rehab center handled other problems besides alcoholism.

In the morning, I went to see the doctor. He took blood tests and a urine test. Then I went back to bed. I had skipped breakfast, but I got up for lunch. The food was good, and I ate quite a lot. I sat with a cool guy named George. Eventually, we would become best friends.

"What was your drug of choice?" I asked him.

"Speed, pot, alcohol," he said, laughing. "What about you?"

"Pot," I said.

"You're here for pot? You've got to be kidding me."

"No, I'm addicted. I can't stay away from the stuff."

"Are you addicted to sex too?" he asked.

"No," I said.

"I am. I love that pussy. There's some good pussy in here."

"I've got a girl back home."

"Where are you from?" he said.

"Syracuse, NY. What about you?" I replied.

"Right around here," he said.

He was very affable and very in control. Everybody liked him, but he wasn't the loud, popular type. He spared his words and hit his target carefully.

After lunch, I went back to bed. They knew about my bipolar disorder, and they wanted me to get some sleep. I got up for dinner and felt a lot better. I sat with George again, and he noted the difference in me.

"You seem a lot more relieved," he said. "It's going to take you a while to get used to being without the pot."

"Yeah, the good thing is I'm not craving it right now, but I am horny as hell."

"Just jerk off a few times a day. That'll take care of you."

"How long have you been here?" I asked.

"I came in a week before you," he said.

"Did you have to detox?" I said.

"For about three days. What about you?" he replied.

"No. The doctor said I didn't have to."

"Good for you. They don't have to put you on Librium or anything?" he asked.

"I'm already on medication."

"For what?" he said.

"I'm bipolar."

"What do they have you on?" he inquired.

"Haldol."

"Never heard of it."

"It releases the nerves and integrates the mind."

"Sounds like good stuff."

"I can't feel it."

We finished eating and went out for a smoke. He was married with three children, but had had other children with two former wives. He was separated now and trying to get back together with his wife.

"Did you see that Laura chick? I'd like to fuck her," he said.

"Yeah, she's hot. What's her story?" I said.

"She has an eating disorder, bulimic, but she's not too thin or anything."

"No, she's just right," I said. "How old is she?"

"Twenty-one," he said.

"There's that Melanie girl too. She's hot."

"Yeah, she has a scumbag boyfriend," he said. "They were heavily into speed before she came in. He doesn't want any help. He's still out there getting fucked up, and she wants to get back together with him."

"She told you that?" I asked.

"She's in my group. Besides, everybody knows everything about everybody else in here."

"How do you like group?" I said.

"It's all right, I guess. I don't think I need therapy, but it helps get things off your chest."

"I haven't been to my group yet. I go tomorrow," I said.

George had a strong faith in God, he explained to me, which I didn't have, and he told me that was the only thing between him and a drug. I figured my personal resolve would have to take the place of faith in a higher power, but he told me it wouldn't work. We talked for another half hour until he had to go to a meeting. I went to bed early that night and got quite a lot more sleep. They woke me up for breakfast, so I dragged my ass out of bed and brushed my teeth. The coffee tasted so good that morning, and my head was clear. I felt much better without the pot and had more energy.

I sat with George, who had a full plate of eggs and bacon. I ate a great deal that morning, and George warned me that it was easy to put on weight in here.

"What time is group?" I asked him.

"Nine thirty, and it lasts an hour and a half."

"Is your wife going to visit you today?" I said.

"No, but my girlfriend is," he laughed.

"How are you going to get back together with your wife if you have a girlfriend?" I asked.

"I'm not worried about it. They know each other too. They used to be best friends."

"How long are you staying here, George?" I said.

"Six months. I'm facing five felonies for guns and dealing drugs, so I have to stay here a long time. I don't care. I like taking a break from work."

"What kind of work do you do?" I asked.

"My family is in the trash business. We have the largest family-owned trash business in the country."

"You must be pretty wealthy."

"I'm not. My family is. What about you?" he said.

"What?" I replied.

"Are you wealthy?" he repeated.

"I've got a trust fund, and my parents are wealthy."

"Lucky you."

"It doesn't help much when all I do is spend it on pot."

"Well, now you don't have to."

"True," I said.

We talked for quite a while and smoked a few cigarettes. It was nice being outside in the fresh air. The ocean smelled great, and the warm wind felt good against my body. Laura came outside to have a cigarette, so George and I went over to talk to her.

"What's up, girl?" George said.

"I haven't met you yet," I said.

"Laura," she said.

"Paul," I said.
"Where are you from, Mr. Paul?" she asked.
"New York," I said.
"Great city," she said.
"No, not the city. Syracuse."
"Small town?" she asked.
"Not really."
"What do you do there?" she said.
"I used to teach at the university. Now I just write and paint."
"What do you write?" she said.
"Novels, poetry, philosophy."
"A man of letters," she said.
"You could say that."
"I'm a student," she said.
"Where?" I asked.
"Texas."
"What are you studying," I said.
"Men."
"Good subject!" I laughed.

I liked her. Not only was she very good-looking, but she was sharp. She had brown hair and big brown eyes. Her hair was pulled back in a ponytail. She had the sexiest legs and ass in the world.

"Are you published?" she said.

"Not yet, but I brought one of my novels with me if you want to read it."

"I'd love to. What's it about?" she said.

"It's about an alcoholic professor who falls in love with one of his students."

"Oh, an autobiography?" she wondered.

"No, it's not actually; pure fiction. He's much older than I am and he's divorced with three children. Besides, I've never fallen in love with one of my students."

"Maybe I could transfer, and you could be my professor," she said.

"We don't have to wait that long," I said.

George was laying back, playing it cool, waiting for his entrance. It never came. We were called in for group, and the three of us separated.

My group was composed of four women and one other man. Our therapist was a woman who was recovering from alcoholism as well. She was great. We did a so-called feelings check in the beginning, and then began talking about our problems.

"How do you feel right now, Paul?" the therapist named Ellen asked me.

"I feel good, hopeful even."

"What else?" she probed.

"That's it."

"Dig deep. There are layers of feelings."

"I have some fear, a little loneliness, and some excitement."

"That's good."

We went around the room, and I noticed there was a lot of depression amongst the women. Once we got talking, the problems began to flow. Most of the women had children, whom they had to give up, or were out of control. On the other hand, I was single, in love, and feeling good about life.

After group, I went to take a little nap. I fell into a deep sleep, and one of the aides had to wake me for lunch. George was sitting with Laura, already eating, when I arrived at the cafeteria.

"How was group?" he asked.

"My God, I never knew people could have so many

problems," I said.

"Yeah, I hate to say it, but the women have a lot of problems."

"So do the men," Laura said.

"We do too, I guess," I said. "What are you here for?"

"An eating disorder. I don't have a problem with alcohol," she said.

I liked her. She was cool and confident. She knew her sensuality made puppets of us men. I wanted to fuck her, but didn't know how to go about it in there.

"What kind of eating disorder?" I said.

"I'm bulimic."

"Are you getting it under control?" I asked.

"Slowly but surely."

"Why do so many women have eating disorders?" I said.

"Who knows," she said.

"They're trying to change themselves into something different and better than they are," George said. "It's low self-esteem."

"That's part of it," Laura said.

"You don't seem to have low self-esteem," I said to Laura.

"Looks are deceiving," she said.

I figured we had better change the subject before someone's feelings got hurt.

"Are you guys going on the beach walk later this afternoon?" I said.

"Sure. That's the best part of the day," Laura said.

"How long does it last?" I said.

"An hour," George said.

I had finished eating, and I wanted to call Linda before she went to school. I excused myself and made my way to the pay phones.

"Hello?" she began.

"Hi, sweetheart," I said.

"Paul! How are you? I miss you so much. How's the place?" she said in quick succession.

"It's fine. I'm having some trouble sleeping, but the people here are great."

"How do you feel?" she asked.

"I have a lot of extra energy. I feel good."

"What am I going to do without my tutor?" she said.

"You'll just have to come out here."

"I'll be out in a few months. I promise."

"We have a beach walk every afternoon. This place really is like a resort. God knows, it costs enough."

"I'm glad. You were worried for a while," she said.

We talked for about half an hour. I felt better after talking to her. I went back to bed to get a little nap before group, and I got up feeling energetic.

Chapter Twenty-One

I adjusted quickly to the routine and started sleeping better at night. That first week, I spent a great deal of time with George and Laura, and I got very close to them. One night, about nine days into my stay, Laura and I planned to sneak out at night and go to the beach.

"What happens if we get caught?" she said.

"We'll be put on restrictions, that's all. They're not going to kick us out. We're paying too much money."

At about eleven o'clock that night, we went outside for a cigarette. A few people were standing with us, so we waited until they went inside. I grabbed Laura's hand and started running for the road that led to the beach. After a block, we slowed down and began to walk.

"This is so exciting," she said. "I love getting into trouble."

"We won't really get into too much trouble. George was telling me about another couple that did it."

"What happened to them?" she said.

"They couldn't be too close to each other after that, but they could talk to each other."

When we got to the beach, we immediately noticed the quarter moon hovering over the water, reflecting diamond speckles on the waves. We took our clothes off and walked a couple of feet into the water. It was freezing.

"So much for that idea," I said.

"Let's make love," she said.

"Gladly!" I said.

We grabbed our clothes and walked to one end of the beach, where we could hide behind some rocks.

"You'll still respect me in the morning, won't you?" she laughed.

"No way!" I teased.

We found a sandy spot and put our clothes down under us. We lay together. It was pretty cold out, so we decided to put some of our clothes back on.

"I wish we could do this in a warm bed," she said.

"I don't have any money, or I'd get us a hotel room," I said.

I started kissing her and massaged her pussy. She got wet pretty quickly, so I got on top of her and put it in. It wasn't exactly a lesson in foreplay. We didn't have much time to deal with. She started moaning right away, and I began thrusting harder, wanting her to come. I was very big that night. She excited the hell out of me.

Suddenly, she said, "I love you."

"I love you too," I said, surprised.

"I want to come in your mouth," I said.

"Okay."

"But I want you to come first," I said.

I got off her and started licking her pussy, putting three fingers inside her. She came after several minutes and screamed out in ecstasy. I rolled on my back, and she went down on me. I told her to suck hard, and soon I came, blowing my load in her mouth. She gagged and spat it out, and we both started laughing.

"I can usually do it," she said.

"It's all right," I said.

"Your come tastes good."

"It's all in the diet."

"We'd better get back," she said.

We were freezing cold as we put our clothes back on. It had been a great adventure, and I didn't care what kind of trouble we got in. When we arrived at the rehab center, two of the night staff were waiting for us. They didn't say much, except to tell us to go back to bed and that the staff would handle it in the morning.

I slept pretty well the rest of the night and woke up early, feeling refreshed. I took a hot shower and dressed for breakfast. George was waiting for me when I arrived.

"Hey, stud, I heard about your little adventure," he laughed.

"Have you seen Laura?" I said.

"She's in talking to a staff member."

I ate breakfast quickly and saw Laura a few minutes after I finished eating.

"Hey, what did they say to you?" I asked.

"They said I have to stay away from you. That's all."

Right after that, the director called me into his office.

"I'm disappointed in you," he said.

"I'm sorry," I said. "I simply couldn't resist the temptation."

"I guess I can understand that. She's a beautiful woman, but you're here to recover from your problems. You don't have to compound them."

"I understand. It won't happen again."

I felt like a little kid being scolded by his father. He told me I was restricted from hanging out with Laura, but that I could talk to her at mealtimes. I went to groups and kept my mouth shut. I just listened to everybody else complain.

A couple of nights later, I called Linda. We talked every other night or so. The phone bills were too expensive to talk every night.

"Hey, what's up?" I said.

"I'm working on this theory paper, and I'm perfectly confused. I need my tutor!" she said.

"When are you coming to visit?" I replied.

"May fifteenth. I already have my tickets. I talked Dad into paying for them."

"That's great! I'll be in the halfway house by then. We can go to the beach and eat at restaurants. It'll be a great vacation for you."

"I love you," she said.

"I love you too."

After I hung up, I was all excited. I tried to take a nap, but I couldn't sleep. I had already forgotten about Laura, but not really. Laura was my companion away from home. She would provide great comfort for my loneliness.

At lunch, I sat with George and Laura as usual. I wanted to tell George about Linda coming, but had to wait until later.

"I relapsed last night," Laura said.

"What do you mean?" I said.

"I threw up."

She had tears in her eyes and her voice quivered. I really couldn't understand it. Why did she feel the need to throw up?

"Why, honey?" I said.

"I don't know. If I knew, I would be cured."

"That's not true either," George said. "Just because you know why doesn't mean you're cured. But you can learn to control it even if you don't know why."

"You've been listening to our lectures," Laura laughed through her tears.

"It's like alcoholism," he said.

"It's an addiction?" I said.

"Not exactly," he said.

"I have to get it under control," Laura said.

"You'll be able to if you stay here for a while and get treated properly," George said.

"I'm trying," she said.

I wanted to help her so badly, but there was nothing I could do. It occurred to me that literature could help someone – besides being entertaining and enlightening, which were the standard purposes of literature. I would write about this someday, I thought, and help myself at the same time. We finished eating, and I went back to bed. I was so grateful that the rehab center was not run like a military school.

Chapter Twenty-Two

A week later, Laura and I were taken off restrictions and were allowed to spend time together. I had told her about Linda, but she didn't care. I think we were falling in love with each other because we were going through a difficult experience. That afternoon when we were taken off restrictions, we went on a beach walk and talked.

"What are you going to do when you get out of here?" she asked.

"Go back to my simple life in Syracuse. I write or paint in the morning and spend the rest of my time hanging out with friends."

"Sounds like a good life."

"I like it. What about you?" I inquired.

"I'll go back to school. I miss my friends. I want to stay in touch with you though."

"We'll stay in touch. I really care for you. I want to see you succeed."

"I feel like I'm making progress."

"I think you're doing great," I said.

I looked out over the ocean and thought about taking a trip to Italy to see my relatives. I wanted to take Laura with me, but I figured we probably would never see each other after rehab. I thought about Linda; I wanted to be with her so badly.

"Maybe we could get married," she said out of the blue.

"Our lives are so far apart," I said.

"I love you, Paul."

"You'll go back to your friends and forget all about me."

"I'll never forget you," she said tenderly.

I wanted to kiss her but couldn't without getting into trouble.

"Maybe we could have a cigarette tonight and kiss a little," I said.

"I'm up for it," she said.

After the beach walk, I took another nap. I was getting used to napping in the afternoon because I was still having trouble sleeping at night. I had talked to my psychiatrist in Syracuse. She asked me if I wanted to increase my medication, but I declined.

That night, I went outside for a cigarette at eleven o'clock. Laura was already there waiting for me. Other clients were smoking, so we waited for them to leave.

"You've got your hair pulled back. It looks good," I said.

"I put some makeup on too."

"Let's go behind those bushes. We have a little time," I said.

We snuck behind the bushes, and I grabbed her immediately. There was no time to waste. I kissed her passionately and put her hand on my cock, which was already hard. She dropped to her knees, unzipped my pants, and began to suck my cock. I was so excited, I came right away, squirting it down her throat. She swallowed it all and said, "Yum."

"You go back first," I said, "just in case."

We smoked some more cigarettes in the heavy Santa Ana winds, and I reflected on my life back in Syracuse. I loved Laura, but she was young and lacked experience. Linda was more worldly and more of a challenge. I kissed Laura goodnight and went to bed. I was tired and glad to hit the pillow. I slept well that night for the first time and got up feeling refreshed. I actually sang in the shower, thinking that my recovery was well on its way.

Two days later, when I got to breakfast, George was pretty upset.

"What's wrong, buddy?" I said.

"My wife wants a divorce."

"Why? You're getting your act together."

"She didn't really give me a reason. She says she's had enough."

"She might change her mind. You're both going through a lot right now."

"I don't think so. She sounded pretty serious."

"Is she coming in to talk to your counselor?" I asked.

"Yeah, but I'm worried she found somebody else."

"Not likely," I said.

He calmed down somewhat as I talked to him. Just then, Laura walked in and sat down.

"What's up, fellas? I feel great this morning!" she beamed.

"I'm glad you are," George said.

"What's the matter?" Laura said.

"My wife wants a divorce."

"Oh no, I'm so sorry."

"She'll get over it," I said.

"Of course she will," Laura said.

We ate in silence for a while. George was almost in tears. I had never seen his cool exterior broken. After breakfast, we went to group, but all I could think about was George. I wondered why anyone would want to break up a marriage when somebody was trying to get help. I was glad that I was single and didn't have to put up with anyone's bullshit. I could start over, unimpeded, with the love and understanding of my family. I didn't really know, of course, what George's wife had been put through, so I couldn't really blame her. There was enough blame to go around, but that wasn't going to solve the problems.

That evening we gathered for dinner, and George was in much better spirits.

"I talked to Karen. She said she might give us another chance; she's coming here for family therapy."

"That's great," I said.

"You're too good a man to give up on," Laura said.

"She's scared, and I don't blame her," George said.

"Family therapy will help," I said. "You'll be able to concentrate on the future instead of dwelling on a difficult past."

"She doesn't think I can stay clean and sober," he said.

"She drinks herself, doesn't she?" I said.

"Yes, but she doesn't think she has a problem."

"It's going to be difficult for you to stay sober if she drinks," Laura said.

"I know, I know," he said, shaking his head.

For the first time in weeks, I felt scared. What if I couldn't stay sober? What if my life continued to go downhill, and I was stuck living alone? The chance of success was very small. I knew that. I would have to succeed. There was no other way.

"You can stay sober, though, even if she drinks. It's possible," I said.

"Doesn't she want to quit," Laura said, "considering all the problems it's caused you?"

"She doesn't want to quit; she doesn't think she has a problem."

"Well, at least you're not in denial," I said.

"Maybe there's somebody out there who is sober, who would be better for you," Laura said.

"I don't even want to think about that," he said.

Now George was getting distraught again; I figured it was better to drop the subject.

"Let's talk about something else," I said.

"Good idea," George said.

We started gossiping about some of the other residents, and soon the laughter was flowing. Laura had a lovely laugh and a great sense of humor. George was very dry and quick with his wit. After breakfast, we split up to go to our respective groups, which allowed me to concentrate again on my recovery.

Chapter Twenty-Three

The days were starting to pass more quickly; at first, time dragged. I could feel myself counting every minute. Now, I was starting to look forward to moving into the halfway house, which was on the same property as the rehab center. I had a week left of being an inpatient, and then I would be free. I was more determined than ever to stay clean and sober, and I began to really enjoy my support group meetings.

At dinner one night, George and I were shooting the shit and noticed that one young lady was about to go crazy.

"I hate this place!" she screamed. "I'm leaving!"

She tipped over a table and made her way to the back door. Nobody tried to stop her. I didn't know her very well. She was a cocaine addict and had only been there a few days. That much I knew. George stood up and calmly followed her out the door. She was walking off the property when George called to her.

"Wait a minute. Let me talk to you," he said.

"I don't know what he said to her, but he brought her back inside after a few minutes. She went right to her room, crying. George sat back down at our table.

"Good for you," Laura said.

"No big deal," George said.

"You should be a counselor," I said.

"I'll stick to the trash business," he said.

We finished eating and went out to smoke. I was really starting to think that I would stay in California. It was so beautiful where we were, and I was making good friends. In a couple of months, Linda would be coming to town, and I thought maybe I could convince her to stay.

That night, I was restless and couldn't sleep. I got up every hour to smoke, worried about everything. The next morning, I was exhausted and asked to be released from group so I could sleep. They gave me a pill, and I went back to bed following breakfast. I slept until lunch and then got up to face the day. George and Laura were already eating when I arrived.

"Rough night?" George said.

"Yeah, I have a lot of things on my mind."

"Like what?" Laura said.

"I don't know if I want to stay in California or go back home."

"Just stay," George said.

"Come to Texas with me," Laura said seriously.

"I don't know if I can stay clean and sober back in Syracuse," I said.

"Here, you're establishing a new network of sober people," he said.

"I know, but I miss my family," I said, thinking about Linda.

"You have time to think about it. Don't lose any sleep over it," Laura said.

After lunch, I took another nap and felt better by dinner. I decided to call Linda. It had been several days since I had spoken to her.

"Hey, what's up, kid?" I said.

"Hi, honey. I miss you so much," she said.

"I miss you too."

"I got a B on a theory paper," she said.

"That's good."

"No, it's not. If you had been here, I would have gotten an A."

"Don't worry about it."

"I'm not really. I'm getting A's in all my other classes."

"Good girl."

We talked for about half an hour. She lifted my spirits considerably. I didn't tell her that I was thinking about staying in California. While I was on the phone, I kept thinking about Laura. I wanted to run away with Laura to Texas and hide from the rest of the world. At that moment, I felt trapped. I couldn't escape into my world of pot, and I couldn't have Laura. I felt scared. I said goodbye to Linda and went to lie down on my bed. I wanted to smoke a joint so badly. After half an hour, I got up from the bed and went to seek out George. He had finished eating and was wondering where I was.

"What's up with you?" he said.

"Right now, I have a terrible craving for pot," I said.

"It'll pass," he said.

"Don't you have cravings?" I asked.

"Sure, but I don't pay any attention to them."

"I wish I could do that."

"You'll be able to eventually."

"How long do the cravings last?" I said.

"A few months; you have to turn your mind to other things."

"Like sex?" I contemplated.

"Well, you don't want to trade addictions, but if you have to, sex is all right."

"That's all I think about now."

"It's not unusual. I think about it a lot too."

He was great. He always made me feel better. Even though he was a couple of years younger than I was, I felt like he was my older brother. I went to bed early that night, as usual, and fortunately fell right to sleep. I woke up a few hours later and went outside for a smoke. Some of the clients were already outside, so we gossiped for a while. The air was cool, and there was a strong breeze. I felt pretty good. After a couple of cigarettes, I went back to bed. As I got through difficult days, I started to feel stronger. I could do this. I knew I could. I would just have to concentrate like hell.

Chapter Twenty-Four

Two days later, George and I got moved into the same halfway house. I was elated. George had a car, so we were mobile. The first thing we did was go to Starbucks to get a really strong cappuccino.

"I feel like I'm getting out of jail," he said.

"All we have to do is stay clean and sober, and we'll feel like that every day," I said.

"When did you say Laura is getting out?" he said.

"I think it's four days," I said, "but she's going to try to sneak out tonight and come over to our place."

We were living in a small three-bedroom cabana. The refrigerator hadn't been defrosted in months, so that was the first thing I did. We went to the grocery store and bought some food, even though we were still on the meal plan. All I could think about was fucking Laura. I was hoping she would be successful at sneaking out. We had a television, but it was usually only background noise.

That night, I sat in front of the TV, waiting for Laura. I could hear the Santa Ana winds blowing through the trees, and it was starting to rain. I was worried that she wouldn't make it, but at eleven thirty, I heard a faint knocking at the door.

"Hi, I don't have much time," she said as I opened the door.

"Come on in. You're soaked," I said.

George was already in bed, but my room was next to his, and the walls were very thin.

"Let's get naked," I said.

"Not tonight. I just wanted to see your place. Let's wait until I get out. I don't want to get in trouble."

"Okay. Well, this is it. There's not much to it."

"It's nice, though. Where's your bedroom?" she asked.

"Right here."

"I can't wait to get out of rehab. Without you and George, it's really boring in there."

"I can imagine."

"I have to go. Give me a kiss," she said.

I put my arms around her and gave her a tender, passionate kiss. I squeezed her ass and gave her a little tap as she went out the door. I slept well that night. I was getting used to being sober. I had frequent dreams of getting high and drunk, which were like small nightmares, but after a while, those dreams subsided.

George and I got up early, feeling good, and we got in his old Mercedes and went to Starbucks. I loved the mornings in California. The birds were always singing, and the sun was always shining. We took our coffees to the beach and hung out for a bit. There were islands off the coast that stood majestically on the ocean.

We had an outpatient program to attend for a couple of hours during the day, but most of our time was for ourselves. George had some money coming in from his family, and my mother was sending me my allowance. George loved cars, so we spent some time going around looking for deals on used cars. Life was good, and I was really starting to think that I would stay in California.

Chapter Twenty-Five

Laura got out four days later and moved into the women's cabana next to ours. That first night, George and I took her out to dinner at a family restaurant not too far away.

"My God, it's great to get out of that place; now we're going to have some fun!" she said.

I watched her eat and noticed she was eating pretty normally. I wondered if it had been a good idea to take her out to a restaurant.

"What have you guys been doing?" she said, interrupting my thoughts.

"We've been hanging out at the beach mostly. We go to Starbucks in the morning, and then we go to our outpatient program. What kind of program do you have?" I said.

"I have to go to group twice a day, but then the rest of the day I'm free."

"How long are you planning to stay?" I said.

"A few months. I'm not sure yet."

After dinner, we drove along the beach and watched the sunset. The orange sky turned dark blue as the sun crept below the surface of the ocean. The water was still, and the orange reflection of the sun stretched to the horizon. I felt happy. I was very glad that I didn't have to be under the influence of any drug to appreciate the sunset and the company of my friends.

I went to bed early as usual, but because I was still a little manic,

I had trouble falling asleep. I probably got four or five hours of sleep that night, but I got up feeling good. I watched the early morning news and waited for George to get up. I had to wait from five to seven, but finally, he got his ass out of bed.

"Come on. Let's go to Starbucks," I said.

"All right. What about Laura?" he said.

"I'll go see if she's up yet."

I walked next door and knocked gently on the door.

Laura opened up and said, "What are you doing up so early?"

"I'm always up early. Do you want to go to the coffee shop with us?" I asked.

"Sure. Let me put some clothes on."

She looked sexy as hell in her pajamas. We all piled into the car and drove away in the early morning light. It felt great to be alive. I was on a pink cloud, excited to be clean and sober and in love again. At the coffee shop, we all ordered double cappuccinos and muffins. Laura devoured her muffin while we were sipping our coffees, and she excused herself to go to the bathroom.

"She's going to throw that up," George said.

"Do you think so?" I said.

"Of course."

I felt naïve and wished that Laura was over her disease, but it wasn't that simple.

"Maybe we should tell her counselor," I said.

"I wouldn't."

"Why not?" I challenged.

"Laura's not going to get better until she decides for herself."

"Yeah, but maybe she needs to be an inpatient a little longer."

When she got back, we didn't say anything. We finished our breakfast and walked outside for a smoke.

"This is the life," Laura said.

She was wearing a short skirt, and her hair was pulled back as usual. She had a tank top on, and her belly was exposed. I stood next to her and grabbed her ass.

"Later," she whispered in my ear.

After our cigarettes, we got in the car and drove back. Laura had to go to her morning group. Then, George and I went to the beach with Melanie, who had been in the halfway house for a week.

Melanie was very sexy too, and George wanted to fuck her. She was very cool and loved to tease George. At the beach that day, she was wearing a thong. She had a lovely ass. She gave George a backrub while we hung out, and the day went by slowly. That night we made a plan to get together with the girls.

The halfway houses were only lightly monitored; the last check was at eleven o'clock, and the counselor lived on the premises. We decided to meet at our house at midnight, and everything went according to plan. The girls came over in their nighties. Melanie was wearing blue, Laura was wearing pink.

"We've got to be perfectly quiet," George said.

We didn't waste any time. Laura came into my room, and Melanie went into George's. The walls were thin, so Laura and I could hear everything that was going on in the other room. But we were making noise ourselves. I ripped her nightie right off her and pulled her panties down around her ankles. She kicked off her panties and pulled my head down into her crotch. I licked and licked as she forced my face into her cunt. I could hardly breathe, so I came up for air.

"Don't stop," she said.

I took off my clothes, and we got into the sixty-nine position. She put my whole cock into her mouth and almost gagged on it.

I stuck my tongue as deep into her pussy as I could, tasting her delicious juices. I was so excited I came into her mouth, and she swallowed it all down. I kept licking her until she came. Then we took a break.

"My God, I've never come so hard in my life," she said.

She started stroking my cock again, but I stopped her.

"Not yet, honey. It's still sensitive."

We could hear George and Melanie going at it, and we pressed our ears against the wall.

"Fuck me up the ass," I could hear Melanie say.

Laura and I started laughing, and we were sure they could hear us.

"Did you ever try that?" I said.

"No, and I don't think I want to."

"Oh, come on. It doesn't hurt,"

"Of course it hurts."

"Let's try it. Then, if it hurts, we'll stop."

"All right."

She got on all fours and stuck her ass way up in the air. I got behind her and rubbed my cock until it got hard. Her ass was so tight, I couldn't fit it in. I didn't have any Vaseline, so I tried to force it in. After several minutes, we decided to give up.

"Next time, I'll have some Vaseline," I said.

"There won't be a next time," she said.

I chuckled a bit and lay on my back. She kissed me and left. Right after that, Melanie came out and said goodbye. George and I had a good laugh afterward, then went to bed satisfied.

The next day, we got up early and went to Starbucks as usual. I was always in a good mood early in the morning.

"What time do you think the princesses will get out of bed?"

I asked George.

"Well, they have group at nine, so probably about eight, eight thirty."

"We should take them to the beach this afternoon and fuck them again."

"That's a very good idea," he said.

When we got back to the house, we discovered that we had a new roommate. His name was Eliot, and he turned out to be a great guy. Eliot had been a captain of the fire department before he got caught dealing drugs. He had had a three hundred dollar-a-day habit, which was killing him. He did eight months in jail and then came to our halfway house. He was shorter than George and I and a few years older. Eliot had jet-black hair and a pleasant face.

"What's up, guys?" he said as we entered.

"Chillin'," George said.

"What do you do for fun around here?" he said with a wink.

"Mostly, we go to the beach and hang out," I said.

"That sounds pretty good," he said.

"We need to find you a girl," George said.

"You guys have girlfriends?" he asked.

"Yup," I said.

"This is starting to look pretty good," Eliot said.

He had a big grin on his face, and I could tell by the way he spoke that he was a really nice guy. The three of us went to the rehab center for breakfast, and Eliot was enthralled by the women in their pajamas.

"This seems like a resort," he said.

"There's a lot of hard work to be done here if one wants to recover," George said.

"I've been sober these last eight months in jail, and I have a support network," Eliot said.

"Then you have a jump on us," I said.

We ate quickly and went out for a smoke. It was another beautiful day in southern California, and I felt great. Melanie and Laura were walking toward the rehab center and spotted us.

"What's up, guys?" Melanie said.

"This is Eliot, our new roommate," George said.

"How do you do, ladies," Eliot said.

"You look like you can keep up with these guys," Laura said with a big smile.

"I was hoping maybe you could fix me up with one of your friends," Eliot said.

"Boy, you don't waste any time, do you?" Melanie said.

"Why put off till tomorrow what you can do today?" Eliot laughed.

"Maybe Chrissy would like to go out with you," Laura said.

"Is she fucked up in the head?" Eliot asked.

"No. She's great. She just had a little drinking problem," Melanie said.

We arranged to get together later in the day, and Eliot was excited about meeting this new woman. We all liked Chrissy and thought she would probably make a good match. Chrissy was about my age, tall and slender. She had a good personality and was fun to be around.

I went back to the house to take a nap while the others hung around and talked. I was in the habit of taking a couple of naps a day, and I didn't care when I took them. In the afternoon, the six of us piled into Eliot's van, went to the beach, and had a good time fooling around. I wanted to get laid but, of course, it was impossible. After the beach, George, Eliot, and I went to a support group meeting, and I listened intently to the messages. I quickly realized that all the others in the group had more serious problems than I did, which surprised me. Even the men and women with a lot of sober time had more problems than I did. If they could stay sober, facing all their problems, then so could I. I felt encouraged, and when I left the meeting, I felt better than I had in a long time.

Chapter Twenty-Six

A few days later, I got up early and jogged along the beach. I felt invigorated and happy to be alive. When I returned to the house, Eliot was making espresso with his new machine.

"Why don't we just go to Starbucks?" I said.

"I want to try this thing out. It'll save us a lot of money," Eliot said.

"We should barbecue tonight," I said.

"Good idea. We'll invite the girls," he said.

"Is George still sleeping?" I said.

"Yeah, he snuck Melanie in last night."

"I didn't even hear them."

"I couldn't get to sleep; they were so loud," he said.

"He had better be careful, or he's going to get caught," I said.

"He doesn't care much at this point," Eliot said.

"Well, he'd better care. He's facing five felonies," I said.

The espresso was done, and Eliot steamed the milk while I cleaned the kitchen. It tasted very good; we had a new chef in our midst and would rely less and less on the cafeteria. The phone rang, and I wondered who could be calling so early. It was Linda.

"Hi, sweetheart," I said.

"You haven't called in a while," she said. "You're a bad boy."

"I meant to call you yesterday, but we're so busy with our groups and other things," I said.

"No excuses," she said.

"When are you coming?" I said.

"I'll be there in two weeks. You'll have to book a hotel for me."

"Okay. Call me in a few days."

"You call me," she said.

"All right."

After I got off the phone, a feeling of fear traveled up my spine, thinking of how Laura would take meeting Linda. Eliot was laughing when I told him of my dilemma.

"What am I going to do?" I asked him.

"Keep them separate as much as you can," he said.

"Laura will be cool about it," I said.

"Maybe, maybe not," he said.

At that point, George stumbled into the kitchen.

"Hey, that coffee smells good," he said.

"It's espresso," Eliot said.

"Who was on the phone?"

"Linda," I said.

"Is she still coming out here?" he replied.

"Yeah, I'm in trouble."

"Tell Laura that you were in love with Linda, but that you're not anymore," George said.

I laughed.

"That easy, huh? I'm going to see if I can live in a hotel for a week. Maybe that'll work."

We sat down and finished our cappuccino. It tasted great.

"Good work, Eliot," George said.

All I could think about was Linda and Laura being really angry with me. Laura knew about Linda, but Linda didn't know about Laura.

"Maybe I should tell Linda not to come out here, and that I'll be back in Syracuse soon.

"She's already got her plane tickets. Don't you want to see her?" Eliot said.

"Of course I want to see her, but what if Laura says something? I don't even know if I want to go back to Syracuse."

"Well, having her come to visit might make up your mind," George said.

"I guess you're right."

I took a shower and got dressed for breakfast. I wanted to talk to Laura and at least reassure her that I wasn't in love with Linda. We went to breakfast, but the three of us ate by ourselves because the girls hadn't gotten out of bed yet.

"What are we doing today, guys?" Eliot said.

"I want to get together with Laura at some point," I said.

"I'm going to the beach," George said.

"I'll join you," Eliot said.

In early recovery, my emotions were perfectly raw. I was stressing over what to do about the women, and I couldn't concentrate on anything.

"What are you going to say to Laura?" Eliot asked.

"I'm not sure, but it'll probably be a lie," I laughed.

"You don't have to lie to her," Eliot said. "You haven't made up your mind. You can tell her that."

"I don't want to lose both of them. I want to be able to choose," I said.

"Maybe having them in the same town at the same time will help you decide," he said.

Everything seemed so clear to everyone else, but I was completely confused. I knew Laura was going back to Texas, which I didn't want to do, but I thought perhaps I could convince her to stay in California. Whenever I was with Linda, I felt in love and at peace, but I hadn't been with her sober, and I didn't know how I would feel.

After the guys left for the beach, I went to the women's house to talk to Laura.

"Hi, sweetheart," I said. "What are you doing today?"

"I have group at nine. Then I'm free. What are you doing?" she replied.

"I guess I'll meet the guys at the beach, but I want to get some writing done at some point."

"Maybe I'll come down to the beach later too."

"Listen, there is something I want to tell you."

"What is it? It sounds serious."

"Linda's coming to town soon. She'll be staying for a week."

"I see," she said.

"I'm confused, Laura. I have really strong feelings for both of you, but my life is in such turmoil. I don't know what to do."

"Well, at least you're being honest about it. Listen, I'll leave you alone while she's here, which will give you time to think about it."

"I appreciate that, and you know I love you."

"It must be tough being in love with two people at the same time," she said.

"It sure is," I said with a smile.

I was relieved immediately, having got that off my chest. Now I could enjoy the rest of the day. I returned to the house and sat down to write. I had decided to write about my rehab experience. There was a wealth of material in front of me. After writing a page, which was my quota, I decided to meet the guys at the beach. The sun was out, and there was a strong breeze coming from the south. The beach wasn't very large in Oxnard, so it didn't take me long to find George's van.

"What's up?" I said to Eliot.

"Nothing. We were just thinking about getting something to eat."

"Sounds good to me," I said.

There was a food stand at the beach, and we ordered hamburgers. I was thinking about Linda coming, and worried that my personality had changed now that I was sober. Of course, it hadn't changed, but that's how I felt. I still wanted to fuck Laura that night, but I knew it was impossible.

"What did you tell Laura?" George asked.

"Basically, the truth – that I'm torn between the two of them and don't know what to do."

"How did she take it?" Eliot said.

"Very well. She appreciated my honesty. I really can't make up my mind."

"Why don't you take one of them and get married? This dating business is maddening," Eliot said.

"I think I could marry Linda. We have a lot to talk about," I said. "On the other hand, Laura and I have great sex."

"It's not about sex," George said.

"I don't think I'm ready to get married," I said.

"First, you have to decide where you're going to live," George said.

We walked back to their spot on the beach, and I lay there in confusion.

"This is nice," I thought. "I could live around the beach and write in the morning."

There were plenty of women around, and I was healthier now that I was sober.

Chapter Twenty-Seven

A week later, Linda arrived. Before seeing her, I wasn't really excited, but the minute she was in my arms, my heartbeat quickened. She looked great with a light tan and her beautiful blonde hair.

"I missed you so much," she whispered in my ear.

"I missed you too," I said.

Our destination was an hour and a half drive up the coast from the airport. We drove along the beach, and Linda was amazed by the sights.

"Would you like to live here?" I finally asked her.

"This is paradise, Paul. I really think I could live here. But can we afford it?" she asked.

"It's cheaper where we're going, and it's almost as nice. We could rent, to begin with, and I could sell the two-family house back home."

Just then, Laura flashed into my mind; I thought about how she would react to this.

"What schools are nearby?" she said.

"Well, there's Santa Barbara, and there are several in LA."

"Oh, I would love to go to Santa Barbara. Is it expensive?" she replied.

"Once you get residency established in this state for six months, it's actually considerably cheaper."

"Oh, it sounds wonderful," she said.

I knew she would be excited once she had seen it, but I was

still faced with my dilemma. I loved Laura too, and I kept thinking about her as I was talking to Linda. Finally, we arrived at the hotel, which was only a few blocks from the halfway house.

"I have some things to do. Why don't you get settled in, take a nap, and I'll call you in two hours."

"Fine. I could use some sleep."

I went back to the halfway house and took a nap myself. I had a funny dream that Linda, Laura, and I were in a sexual threesome. I woke up and laughed to myself. We had talked about having a sense of humor in our support groups, and I was glad that I hadn't lost mine.

I wanted Linda to meet my friends, so the four of us planned to go out for dinner. We picked Linda up at six o'clock; the guys were curious to get a look at her. She wore a white dress and her hair was pulled back the way I liked it.

"I've heard a lot about you two," she said as she got in the car.

"Not as much as we've heard about you," Eliot said.

"How do you like California?" George said.

"It's absolutely gorgeous. I love the beach and the ocean."

"Paul is thinking about staying out here," George said.

"I haven't made up my mind," I said.

"We might live here together," she said.

George and Eliot looked at each other, but Linda didn't notice.

"It's expensive, but it's worth it," George said.

"What do you guys do?" Linda asked.

"I'm a retired fireman," Eliot said. "I think I'm going to go into counseling next."

"I work for my father in the trash business," George said.

"I'm still a student," Linda said. "I'm thinking about going into teaching."

"That's excellent," Eliot said.

"She would be a great writer," I said.

"How many more years do you have to go?" Eliot asked her.

"It depends. I might want to get my Ph.D., so I'd be in school for a long time."

"We have some excellent schools in California," George said.

"Yes, Paul was telling me," she said.

We talked throughout the rest of the dinner, and everybody was getting along fine. I thought about Laura, but not much. I was too involved in our discussion. We took Linda back to the hotel at about nine o'clock and went back to the house.

"She's great, Paul. I don't even know why you're looking elsewhere," George said.

"I'm not well," I said seriously.

"You'd better think long and hard about what you're doing," Eliot said.

"I am."

"Why don't you ask Linda to marry you and be done with it?" George said.

"I might," I said.

I didn't really want to talk about my problems, so I walked into my room and lay on my bed. I couldn't fall asleep; I tossed and turned instead, thinking a lot of negative thoughts. Finally, I got up, turned on the TV, and lit a cigarette in the house, which was against the rules. Eliot and George didn't say anything. They didn't really care about the cigarette. They were more concerned about my well-being.

"Having trouble sleeping?" George said.

"Yeah."

"You're not your usual cheerful self," Eliot said to me.

"I'm not feeling well," I said.

I didn't want to talk about anything; I only wanted to stare at the television until I fell asleep. I thought about Laura and Linda and figured I had better stay with Linda. I knew I would change my mind the next day, but that's how I felt then.

"Why don't you take a hot bath? That usually works for you," Eliot said.

"I think I will."

I got in the hot water and tried to relax. My thoughts were racing. I couldn't stop thinking about the girls, and I wanted to sneak over to Laura's house and fuck her. I went to bed again, and it took me two hours to fall asleep. I woke up several times during the night but, fortunately, was able to fall right back to sleep.

Chapter Twenty-Eight

I slept later than usual and missed going to Starbucks with the guys. I had some toast for breakfast and called Linda.
"Hi, sweetheart. Are you up yet?" I said.
"Yes, I've been up for about an hour. I didn't want to call you because I didn't know how long you'd be sleeping."
"I had a terrible time getting to sleep last night."
"You're not used to falling asleep without the pot," she said.
"That's right, but some nights are better than others."
"What are we doing today?" she said.
"There's not much to do around here, except go to the beach. Listen, do you want me to include you in family therapy?" I asked.
"What is it exactly?" she said.
"Well, I haven't been in it yet, but basically, it's a group setting where everybody works on issues."
"We're not really family though," she said.
"Of course, but they might let me include you."
"I'm up for it," she said.
I was glad that she wanted to get involved in the therapy because there was so much to understand, and it wasn't a matter of just explaining something.

George and Eliot returned shortly, and we packed up to go to the beach. Linda was ready when we arrived at the hotel.
"What a beautiful day!" she said.

It's always like this," I said.

"You two should move to California," Eliot said. "You can go to the beach every day."

"I think I could get used to it," Linda said.

We sat on the beach for a couple of hours. The water was still too cold to swim in, but we got our feet wet. There was a strong breeze from the south, which was warm and dry. I was very much in love and wanted some stability in my life. I thought that I might ask Linda to marry me; my feelings were that strong. I was beginning to feel more confident every day that I could stay clean and sober with the help of my friends.

We went home for lunch, and I showed Linda our modest little house.

"This isn't bad at all," she said.

"It's home," I laughed.

The guys went out somewhere and left the two of us alone.

"Listen, Linda," I said, "I've been thinking about it. Why don't we get married?"

"I'll have to think about it," she said evenly.

"What's there to think about?" I persisted.

"Well, I have to get used to your new personality."

"My new personality? What are you talking about?" I startled.

"You're a bit different now."

"Different, really, how?" I said.

"Just a little. You're quieter, and you don't joke around as much."

"That's good, isn't it?" I asked.

"I'm not saying it's bad. It's just different, that's all. I didn't mean to hurt your feelings."

"You didn't hurt my feelings," I said.

She had hurt me though. I wasn't really willing to admit it. We didn't say anything to each other for a minute, and I could feel my heart racing. I had never thought that there was a possibility of losing her, but that possibility was very real now. I made a pot of coffee and sat down. My thoughts were racing. I even thought that I would dump Linda and go with Laura.

"I'm flattered that you asked me though," she said.

"That's great," I said.

Now I felt very uncomfortable. I didn't know what to say.

"Maybe I should walk you back to the hotel," I finally said.

"Don't be like that. I said I'd think about it, didn't I?" she said.

I could feel the anger welling up inside me. I wanted to yell at her, but I didn't.

"Come on. Let's go," I said.

I walked her back to the hotel and wished she were taking a plane back to Syracuse the next day. Her visit was not turning out the way I had planned, but I told myself that I had to stay calm. I wanted to smoke some pot right then, but a few minutes later, after I dropped her off, the desire passed.

Chapter Twenty-Nine

That afternoon, I took a nap, but I was very restless. I thought more and more about Laura that afternoon and went to her house to see her.

"Hi," I said sullenly.

"What's the matter with you?" she said. "Your girlfriend is here. You should be happy."

"Well, I'm not."

"What happened?" she said.

"I asked her to marry me, and she said she'd think about it."

"So? That's what we all say. We can't be an easy catch. Don't worry about it. She still loves you."

I wanted to tear Laura's clothes off, but figured since Linda was in town, she wouldn't go for it. I was frustrated and wanted to talk to Linda again, but Laura's words soothed me. It was too early in recovery to go through such turmoil, and I was extremely sensitive.

"I know she loves me, but that's not enough. I want her to marry me."

"She will. You've got to give her time. She just got here. Did you make love to her yet?" she asked.

"No, I haven't had the chance."

"The next time you make love to her, ask her again. That should work."

"You really think so?" I said.

"I'm sure of it."

"I guess that means you don't want to make love to me," I said.

"Don't be silly," she said.

"I still love you too, Laura."

I knew I was getting myself in trouble, but I didn't care.

"I love you too, Paul, but you're committed to your girlfriend."

"I'm not so sure anymore."

"Don't give up."

"You're great, Laura. You know that?" I said.

"I know."

I felt like a fool, and my frustration was increasing. Now that I was talking to Laura, I wanted to marry her. I thought about Linda sitting by herself in the hotel room, and I decided I had better call her.

"I'll see you later. I'm going to get together with the guys. They always make me feel better.

"I do really love you, Paul. If things don't work out with Linda, I'll be here for you."

"Thanks, Laura. You're really wonderful. I love you too."

I walked next door to our house and found the guys munching on some potato chips and watching the television.

"Where's Linda?" George asked.

"She's at the hotel," I said.

"You guys getting together for dinner?" Eliot said.

"I don't know," I said.

"You seem kind of down. What happened?" Eliot said.

"I asked her to marry me, and she said she had to think about it."

"It's not a no. She'll agree to it. You've got to give her some time," George said.

"That's what Laura said."

"You just went to talk to Laura?" George said.

"Yeah."

"You really want to fuck things up, don't you?" Eliot said.

I felt like shit and the guys weren't helping. I decided I had better call Linda. I didn't want her to think I was upset.

"Hey, what's up?" I said.

"Oh, this place is so beautiful, Paul. I took a walk on the beach and fed the seagulls.

"Yeah, it's nice, isn't it?" I said.

"Can you come to get me?" she said.

"Yes, but I'll be walking. George needs his car."

"Okay," she said.

"I'll be there in half an hour," I said.

We were already back to normal as if nothing had ever happened. Of course, I was exaggerating everything in my own head, but now I felt better. I took a shower and put on a clean pair of jeans. I was horny as hell and figured maybe she would let me fuck her. When I got to the hotel, she was wearing these really short white pants and a halter top. She looked really hot, and she had some color from the beach. I grabbed her and started kissing her. She was into it, and pretty soon we were naked. I rolled her over and fucked her from behind, my anger making me thrust really hard. She was making a lot of noise, and I knew I was getting to her. After I fucked her, she blew me until I came in her mouth, the way I liked. Now it was my turn to give her an orgasm.

I put one finger in her cunt and began rubbing her g-spot. Then, I ran circles around her clit with my tongue. She was getting wild. As she started to come, I slowed down.

"Don't stop. Don't stop," she screamed.

"Will you marry me?" I said.

"Yes! Yes! Just don't stop!" she gasped.

"All right then," I said, finishing her off.